This diary belongs to: Alistair Fury

For some people Christmas is good: people who think up bad jokes for crackers, people who grow tinsel, people who murder turkeys, people who write modern carols that nobody knows the tune to, people who like eating and eating till their stomachs burst all over the table like big bags of maggots . . .

Christmas should not be about money. Christmas should be a time for sharing and caring. A time to think about all those unlucky people who can't enjoy Christmas. Dead people. People without a telly. Vegetarians.

Read on to share a unique Christmas with Alistair, the Fury family and the Revengers. Another hilarious instalment in *The War Diaries of Alistair Fury* from award-winning writer, Jamie Rix.

www.kidsatrandomhouse.co.uk

Other titles in THE WAR DIARIES OF
ALISTAIR FURY series, published
in Corgi Yearling:

Bugs on the Brain
Dead Dad Dog
Kiss of Death

And for younger readers,
published inYoung Corgi:

One Hot Penguin
Mr Mumble's Fabulous Flybrows

Also available from Jamie Rix:

Grizzly Tales for Gruesome Kids
More Grizzly Tales for Gruesome Kids
Fearsome Tales for Fiendish Kids
Ghostly Tales for Ghastly Kids
Johnny Casanova – the unstoppable sex machine
The Changing Face of Johnny Casanova
The Fire in Henry Hooter
A Stitch in Time
Free the Whales
The Vile Smile
The Last Chocolate Biscuit
Looking after Murphy

THE WAR DIARIES OF ALISTAIR FURY

TOUGH TURKEY

JAMIE RIX

Illustrated by Nigel Baines

CORGI YEARLING BOOKS

For Helen and Jacky with love

THE WAR DIARIES OF ALISTAIR FURY: TOUGH TURKEY
A CORGI YEARLING BOOK : 0 440 864798

Published in Great Britain by Corgi Yearling Books,
an imprint of Random House Children's Books

This edition published 2002

1 3 5 7 9 10 8 6 4 2

Copyright © Jamie Rix, 2002
Illustrations © Nigel Baines, 2002

Papers used by Random House Children's Books are natural,
recyclable products made from wood grown in sustainable
forests. The manufacturing processes conform to the
environmental regulations of the country of origin.

Set in 12/14.5pt Comic Sans by Falcon Oast Graphic Art Ltd.
Corgi Yearling Books are published by
Random House Children's Books,
61–63 Uxbridge Road, London W5 5SA,
a division of The Random House Group Ltd,
in Australia by Random House Australia (Pty) Ltd,
20 Alfred Street, Milsons Point, Sydney, NSW 2061, Australia,
in New Zealand by Random House New Zealand Ltd,
18 Poland Road, Glenfield, Auckland 10, New Zealand
and in South Africa by Random House (Pty) Ltd,
Endulini, 5A Jubilee Road, Parktown 2193, South Africa

THE RANDOM HOUSE GROUP Limited Reg. No. 954009

A CIP catalogue record for this book is available from the
British Library.

Printed and bound in Great Britain by
Cox and Wyman Ltd, Reading, Berkshire

My Daily Diary

This diary belongs to Alistair Fury

Age 11

Address 47 Atrocity Road, Tooting, England

Mobile Phone Number Dnt hv 1

e-mail address don't h@ve one

Club Revengers (secret). Ralph and Aaron are like my brothers except in this one respect: I like Ralph and Aaron, whereas my real brother I don't. He is like a hornet in a car on a long journey. You can't take your eyes off him for a second in case he stings you and he MUST be squashed.

Bank Details It is a big building in the high street where money is kept. The people inside always smile, because they've got all your money. The outdoor doors open into a glass cupboard ONLY when the indoor doors are closed. This glass cupboard is to stop bank robbing. Also, in the hot weather it is a convenient place to bake bread. If it was a spaceship it would be the de-contamination area where you would have to sit for six hours reading comics and eating Mars Bars while all the bugs on your space-walking suit got zapped.

5

Religion All religions preach love and forgiveness, and I don't agree. Smack back first and pray they don't find you later is my motto. My religion is looking after Numbero Uno. Instead of kissing prayer mats I kiss mirrors a lot...

Blood Type Red.

Allergies To my big brother and big sister. If they are even within five metres of me I feel sick and have a violent reaction.

Important birthdays Me and Jesus. His = December 25. Best day of the year.

Notes

For some people Christmas is good: people who think up bad jokes for crackers, people who grow tinsel, people who murder turkeys, people who write modern carols that nobody knows the tune to, people who like eating and eating till their stomachs burst all over the table like big bags of maggots.

WANTED
FOR TURKEY
MURDER

← Turkey in disguise

For some it is bad. Mum and Dad hate Christmas, because their children, cost them an arm and a leg and another arm and a few fingers as well. *that's me, William and Mel* They say that we are like little money vampires bleeding them of money. They say the cost of children is like having a one-armed bandit in the corner of the sitting room. You put in tons more money than you ever get out.

But listen up, parents. Christmas should not be about money. Christmas should be a time for sharing and caring. A time to think about all those unlucky people who can't enjoy Christmas. Dead people. People without a telly. Vegetarians. Vicars. Overpaid footballers who have to work on Boxing Day. And unlucky people stuck on desert islands with no access to a calendar. By mistake, they probably celebrate Christmas in July and NEVER know. Except they *would* know, because there wouldn't be any presents in their stockings, because Father Christmas would still be on his summer holiday, wouldn't he?

But for me, Christmas is brilliant because I get loads of presents.

P.S. Did I mention that I hate my big brother and sister?

DECEMBER 18

7 days to Christmas

TODAY'S TV

BBC2, 10.30: Twerpies

Sports 1, 11.30: Xtreme Conkers

C5, 13.30: Quizmaster Funk

Yoof Channel, 16.00, 16.30, 17.00, 17.30: Bunty the Mozzie Slayer

BBC1, 19.30: When Dinosaurs Walked in Cleethorpes

ITV, 20.30: TV's Rudest **** Off-Cuts!

Groovy Movie Channel, 22.00: Six Cents!

I love Christmas. I love the way it comes round every year whether you like it or not. I love the lights and watching the telly, and the log fires and turkey and shopping in the dark. But most of all I love Father Christmas, because that is the neatest job. He's loved by everyone in the world, he only works one day a year, and he drives a magic sleigh which can loop the loop fifty times quicker than the Spiral-Spew-Looper at

Thorpe Park. And this sleigh is pulled by flying, talking reindeer! They are also fart-free, which is a blessing if you're sitting right behind them.

Rudolf!!!

Today Mum and I performed the ceremony of the Stirring of the Christmas Pudding. We buried money in it. William did it last year but buried the money in his pocket instead of in the pudding, and when Mum said, 'This pudding seems a bit light,' he panicked. He added extra weight to the pudding by bulking it out with his dirty rugby socks. When the rugby socks were extracted at the Xmas dinner table I got the blame, of course, until everyone remembered that I don't play rugby because I'm a coward. As I recall, the pudding had that vomitatious tang of sweat. Mind you, the socks came out clean,

Only a deranged five-bellied pig would appreciate banana kidneys with aniseed tofu balls.

---

which was a bonus. As Granny Constance said seventy-three times, 'That's the wonder of steaming for you.'

William came in to stick his finger in the mix, but Mum told him to go away. 'Alistair is Mummy's Little Helper this year,' she said.

'Thief!' I shouted, hiding behind Mum's apron.

'Creep!' he said.

'Alistair is not a creep,' said Mum. 'He's lovely. He still believes in Christmas, which is more than can be said for you and Melanie, William.'

'I've wrapped my presents already,' I said. 'And this year they're the best ever.'

'See,' said Mum. 'And Alistair appreciates my cooking.'

WHOA! Stop this bus full of people saying loving things about each other! I want to get off! I wouldn't go as far as 'appreciate'. I eat her food, because otherwise I'd starve, but I don't appreciate it. I appreciate looking at

Pamela Whitby, but then she's a dish of quite a different sort!

'Only Alistair understands what a super-human effort it takes to get this house looking nice for Christmas Day,' said Mum.

'He understands what it takes to get a bigger Christmas present,' sneered William.

'Go away,' said Mum, 'and put some clothes on.' William had come straight from his bath to show off his verruca. 'I don't want to see it,' she told him.

'But it's funny,' he said. 'You know how sometimes clouds can look like sheep, or carrots look like two people doing it in a lift, well my verruca looks just like Mr E's bottom.' Mr E is our ugly pug dog whose bottom is not very pretty. It's prettier than his face, but then so is everything in the world, from warthogs to Luke

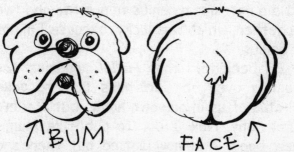

↑ BUM   FACE ↑

Chadwick. William stormed off while I flicked V signs at him behind Mum's back. V for Victory, V for Verruca and V for 'Go boil your head in a vat of worms, loser!'

Then Mum dropped her bombshell. 'I'm going to let you into a secret,' she said, 'seeing as how much you like my food.' She took a cookery book out of the drawer. 'This is my new one,' she said. It's called Celia Fury Cooks Her Goose at Christmas. It's in all good bookshops now, priced twenty-nine pounds ninety-nine p.'

'Goose?' I said suspiciously. 'Christmas?' It did not take a genius to put two and two together, which was lucky, because I'm not a genius.

I'd been told that *Hello!* magazine was coming over on Christmas Day to take photos of us in our own home, but I didn't know why. Now I do. To publicize Mum's new book. And now I find out there's a

It's five.

I love turkey!

catch! No turkey. No succulent, juicy-breasted, drumstick-licking, worth-the-torture-of-a-year-long-wait turkey.

'We're having a goose-tastic Christmas this year,' Mum said in her sad Youth-TV presenter voice. 'Pâté de foie gras with melba toast. Roast goose, with polenta, celeriac, porcini mushrooms and sprouts. Followed by Christmas pud and goose-berries.'

'Which part of the goose are the berries?' I asked nervously. Dangleberries, apparently, wherever they might hang.

do you mind?

Mum saw the look of disappointment on my face. She knows how much I love turkey. 'Not everything's changed,' she said defensively. 'I've kept sprouts on the menu.'

'I hate sprouts,' I said.

13

Treachery! Betrayal! My mother was a Christmas Judas! It was a thunder-mungous shock to find out that a precious cornerstone of my childhood,* something that had been one thing for eleven years, was suddenly going to be something completely different.

'It's no big deal,' said Mum. 'It's goose for turkey – so what? There's a photographer here on Christmas Day – yawn, yawn! Nothing important's going to change, Alistair.'

← **OH YES IT IS!**

'Oh no it's not!' I love arguments in pantomime, because they're so true and life-like that it makes me want to join in. And by that I DO NOT mean that I want to put on a bra and lipstick and kiss Buttons like a Dame!

NOT FIT was once lapped in the 100 metres sprint

Here's proof. Instead of making the stuffing for the turkey like he usually does, Dad went off to the gym to tone himself

14

I am seriously wondering if somehow I am not related to Mother Theresa of Calcutta seeing as how much I'm NOT concerned with money. Maybe I am a Saint and don't know it. Must ask doctor to check for halo next time I'm in.

up for the Hello! photos. He said he was fed up with running a leisure centre and wanted to be discovered and turned into a supermodel. Every model in the world would have to be dead before Dad got a mod-elling job, unless it was modelling swimming trunks for baby hippos with big fat bellies.

Mel has changed too. For the first time ever she's taken a job over Christmas. It's only for three weeks until school starts again, but it's still a job. It's still caring more about MONEY than Christmas.

Mel is working as an elf at Thomas Brothers department store, selling tickets for Santa's Grotto. If I was an elf I'd be furious that a grumpy no-brain like my sister was impersonating me. Elves are pretty creatures with nimble fingers that can make toys. Mel's got clumsy dinosaur bones and a ring through her nose like a bull. (Because she's sixteen now and Mum and Dad can't stop her!) Apparently, she's too grown up for Christmas this year.

'So count me out!' she said. 'It's all so boring. And I'm cutting out food too, in solidarity with our starving cousins in the Third World.'

'And not because you don't want to look fat in that skimpy red dress you've bought to look sexy in the *Hello!* photos on Christmas Day?' I said.

'Tell him to shut up,' she said to Mum, who asked her what had brought this on.

'Gabriel,' I said. Mel looked daggers at me. 'He's the new Christmas postman. He's twenty-five and she thinks he's gorgeous! That's why she's always late for work. She hangs about in the window making gooey eyes at him through the glass. He probably thinks you've got conjunctivitis.'

Mel lunged at me, but Mum held her off. 'Well, tell him to stop!' Mel said.

'Why?' I said. 'Scared you won't get to handle his packages?'

Mum said that that was enough, but I'd only just started. Mel was the enemy. By being older and joyless she was ruining my Christmas! 'Tell me,' I said, 'is it true you only like him because he's got a huge sack?'

Mel ran wailing through the house while I was relieved of pudding duty and sent to my room.

I never made it. My big brother and sister ambushed me on the landing, rolled me up in a rug and chucked me out with the rubbish. Apparently, this was where I belonged. I protested and said things like, 'But 'tis the season of goodwill to all men!' and, 'Peace and love, brother and sister!' and, 'Help!!!' But it had no effect. They tied rope round both ends of the rug and pulled it tight, then propped me up against the front wall with a sign pinned to the rug:

I AM A GIANT
CHRISTMAS CRACKER.
PLEASE PULL ME TILL I EXPLODE
INTO LOTS OF LITTLE BITS.
UNFUNNIEST JOKE IN THE WORLD
INSIDE. I think they meant ME! Ho-ho!!

They left me there. Most passers-by ignored my cries for help, a couple of tramps ran off to rejoin Alcoholics Anonymous, thinking they'd just heard voices, Napoleon (our no-tailed cat) used me as a scratching post and Mr E decided I was a talking tree and cocked his leg on me. Now, I don't know what that pug dog manufactures inside his bladder but it isn't pee. It's acid. Five minutes after he'd drained his worm there was a steaming hole in the rug. It gave me a chance to escape. I sang 'Yellow River' several times to get him to pee again so the hole would get bigger and I could crawl out, but he had nothing left to give. So I stuck my foot out of the hole and waved it up and down in the hope that some kind soul would see my sole and save it.

Luckily, Dad was staggering back from the gym, where he'd just put his back out. Not on the heavy weights, but taking his

socks off in the changing room. It took him ages to release me because of the excruciating pain he was in, and when I finally saw daylight again, a tiny white insect flew out of my hair. I have Christmas moths, which just about sums up my luck right now.

Official Unfunniest Joke in the World

Actually the unfunniest joke in the world is NOT me. It is this:

Knock Knock.
Who's there?
Alistair.
Alistair Who?
Precisely. Who is he? A nobody

← Tumbleweed moment

19

Only two morons sharing the genetic make-up of an orang-utan (e.g. my big brother and sister) find it remotely funny.

Needed revenge. Went inside to phone Revengers for help, only to find home-made horror movie waiting for me on the stairs.

'This,' said Mel, 'is for being Mummy's favourite!'

'Her creepy Christmas helper!' added William. Both of them had my presents in their hands. The ones I'd spent *six months* choosing and *four hours* wrapping!

'Don't do it!' I shouted, but I was too late.

In less than ten seconds all my best

work was undone. They tore open my presents and called out,

'Mum! Alistair's bought you pigs' trotters for your exotic recipes.'

'Dad! Alistair's bought you a tie. Yawn yawn!'

'Melanie! Alistair's bought you a photo album.'

'Already got one, William.'

'Thought you had! What have I got?'

'William! Alistair's bought you a rugby jockstrap!'

I felt like my babies had just been snatched away from me. For a moment I stopped breathing with the horror of everyone knowing what my presents were, but it didn't last long. Three seconds later I took my next breath and ran into the kitchen to find Mum and Dad.

Dad was lying on the table having his back rubbed with embrocation oil. Mum stopped when I came in and Dad wiped the dolphin smile off his face.

'Enough now,' she said, rolling Dad off the table.

'That's the last exercise I'm ever taking,' said Dad, as he put the oil in the fridge and staggered through to the sitting room to watch telly. 'From now on my pursuit of the Body Beautiful will be entirely cosmetic – hair-dye and fake tan!'

Mr E scampered after him, trying to dance the bump with his leg. That embrocation oil must have something in it that makes ugly dogs think they're sexy when they're not.

I asked Mum if she'd heard what William and Mel had just done to me, and if she agreed that they deserved to be pinned out naked on a mountainside for wolves to eat their livers and ears? She said it didn't matter.

'Of course it matters!' I wailed. 'The whole fun of presents is not knowing what they are.'

'The whole fun of presents,' said Mum, plunging her hands into a bowl of chopped red meat, 'is giving them.'

'What's that?' I asked.

'Stuffing,' she said.

'But we always have chestnut stuff-ing,' I moaned. 'And Dad always makes it.'

'He won't handle horse,' she said.

'Horse!' I gasped. 'HORSE!'

'Horsemeat stuffing for the goose,' she said.

'Since when did we have horsemeat stuffing on Christmas Day?' I cried.

'Since I put it in my book,' said Mum. 'So you're saddled with it, Alistair. Ha ha!'

It was not funny. There was a con-spiracy at home to ruin my Christmas and it had worked. My festive hopes had been dashed. The joy of life had been sucked out of me. Christmas as I knew it was DEAD! No turkey, no chestnut stuffing, no presents! I locked myself into my room, ripped down my decorations and flung open my window. 'Good riddance!' I screamed, as I tore up my tainted presents and hurled them into the front garden, where they squelched down into the sucking mud. 'Goodbye Christmas!' I howled. Then I flung myself into bed and tried as hard as I could to cry, because I felt I deserved to. But nothing came out. I was as dry as a manger.

22.50 Day of disappointments. Had no time to watch TV either. Must try harder tomorrow. TV and Christmas go together like God and Jesus, Mary and Joseph, Dolce and Gabbana.

TV MISSED
BBC2, 10.30: Twerpies
Sports 1, 11.30: Xtreme Conkers
C5, 13.30: Quizmaster Funk
Yoof Channel, 16.00, 16.30, 17.00, 17.30: Bunty the Mozzie Slayer
BBC1, 19.30: When Dinosaurs Walked in Cleethorpes
ITV, 20.30: TV's Rudest **** Off-Cuts!
Groovy Movie Channel, 22.00: Six Cents!

03.45 Woke with a start. Climbed on chair and took out small rectangular gift-wrapped box from top cupboard. Put under pillow and slept with it near to my lips, where I knew it was safe. It is a bracelet for Pamela Whitby. It cost me fifteen tokens from Nutty-Mallow-Honey-Chocco-Fruit Flakes. One token per box. That made fifteen boxes to collect. With only three weeks before the offer closed I had to eat five boxes a week: 'Greater love hath no man.'

Greater amount of sick hath no man neither.

DECEMBER 19
6 days to Christmas

TODAY'S TV
BBC2, 10.15: Snothunters
Many-mini-movie Channel, 13.15:
Brownie Badge of Honour
C4, 16.00: Dr Soulfighter and the Curse of
Dragon's Rock
BBC1, 19.00 This Is Your Lie
ITV, 19.30: Who's Been Maimed?
ITV, 20.00: Wham! Bam! Crash! Police
Accident!
C5, 22.30: Ibiza Eater

06.15 Woken by car door slamming. Mel is sitting in the driver's seat of Dad's car. She has switched on the engine and is just sitting there, not moving. Not entirely surprised. She can't drive.

But why?

06.16 There is a pig's trotter sticking out of the mud. Somebody has buried a pig in our front garden!

But why?

06.17 Just remembered what I did last night with my presents.

Why? Oh why? Oh why? Oh why? Oh why? Oh why? OH WHY?

06.28 Phoned Revengers and called emergency meeting to discuss my

Christmas catastrophe. Aaron's mother was quite polite about the early hour of the call. Ralph's father called me a 'fungal foot rotten barn swivelling coat'. If I knew what he meant I might be offended.

07.30 Early breakfast. Mel still in car. William still asleep. Dad still trying to swing legs out of bed with stiff back. For someone trying to make himself look younger than he really is, Dad has made himself look older than Granny. I bet she could beat him at arm-wrestling now.

Mum, was pre-cooking and freezing her polenta. She asked me how I was feeling after my flounce last night. I could barely speak to her after her turkey betrayal, but I managed a whisper through gritted teeth: 'Goose juice makes you loose, you moose!' I sneered and left it at that. I think she got where I was coming from.

Left to meet Revengers. The pig's trotter in the front garden had been chewed by a wild animal. Probably a bear or a wolf or the Beast of Tooting Bec Common!

I thought polenta was something that comes out after a baby is born. I know for a fact that some mad people eat it in France (they eat anything over there), but not on Christmas Day, surely?

SQUEAK
grrrrr...

Or maybe just a fox. Talking of beasts, Mel was still sitting in the car.

When Gabriel came round the corner with his little red trolley I realized why. She switched off the engine and leapt out in front of him – only she kept her back to him so that she could pretend to bump into him as he passed.

'Sorry,' she said, shutting the car door like she owned it. That was it! She wanted Gabriel to think it was her car and she was old enough to drive. But she isn't. She's only sixteen.

'Morning, Melanie,' I said as I pushed between her and Gabriel. 'Mummy was wondering, now that you can miraculously drive before you've even had any lessons, which your parents will be giving you for your seventeenth birthday present, if you could give me a lift into town?' And I got into the passenger seat.

She went bright red and laughed nervously. 'I am seventeen,' she said to him. 'In fact I'm eighteen, and that's true. But I don't know who that boy is at all. Get out of my car, you ruffian! Oh save me, save me, save me!' I think she was hoping Gabriel might save her, but he just looked confused. 'God!' said Mel, trying to sound like a grown-up. 'Don't you just hate home-less orphans! That must be who this boy is. If I had a gun I'd shoot him and I wouldn't care.'

I got out of the car and smiled at Gabriel. 'I'm her little brother,' I said.

'Oh,' said Gabriel in such a way that I could tell that he was a little brother too. 'Respect.'

Revengers met in the second-floor loos at the Thomas Brothers department store

or, as us Revengers call it, on account of its snotty customers, Toss-Bros. This was the loo at the back of Santa's Grotto or, as us Revengers call it, Toss-Bros-Snoss-Gross. Our reasoning was thus:

1) We couldn't use loos at school, because school was closed for the holiday.
2) If we got caught hanging our OUT OF ORDER sign on the Toss-Bros-Snoss-Gross loo door, we could say we were with the elf, Melanie Fury, and they'd definitely let us off, because she's doing an important job for Father Christmas, and he's the most important famous person in the world at this time of the year.
3) We didn't want to meet in the park, because there are millions of geese there

and geese are not my favourite animals right now. Apart from tasting horrible, their poo gets right up the tread of your trainers and sometimes sneaks round the edge like Invading Green Gunk from Outer Space.

INTERESTING FACT

Since we have been meeting secretly in the Toss-Bros-Snoss-Gross loos and working the OUT OF ORDER scam, there have been more damp children sitting on Father Christmas's leg than ever before. But Father Christmas is too nice to complain. He just straps a plastic bag round his knee under the cos- tume and repels moisture silently.

Sometimes it helps me to understand things if I write them down.

First things first. We decided to have a new secret password for Christmas. The secret of a secret password is to make the password 'everyday' so that non-club people don't get suspicious and think, Hello. Why's that remarkably handsome boy using a word that sounds suspiciously like a secret password? If the wrong person was to jump to that conclusion, that could be the end of the secret society. So, for example, a secret password such as 'I say, special chums, let's go for a swim in the boating lake' couldn't possibly work in the middle of winter, when the boating lake is frozen over.

We sat in silence for ten minutes trying to think of an everyday phrase.

'Got it,' said Aaron. *'Hello. How are you?'*

It was certainly everyday, but rather

too much. If we'd chosen 'Hello. How are you?' as our password, our membership would have expanded in one weekend from three to every single English-speaking person on the planet!

WORLD REVENGER CONVENTION

Hi, I'm Bob, Revenger No 1377421

'I've baked the chinchilla,' was another suggestion, but tricky to slip into conversation without some do-gooder phoning the RSPCA. And not very Christmassy either, unless you're a rodentarian – that's a person who prefers eating chinchilla to turkey.

We all liked Aaron's next one, 'You bet I'll have an eggnog!' until Ralph remembered what 'eggnog' meant. Apparently, it's something grown-ups do at office parties with pickled eggs and snogging. So that was definitely out.

In the end we settled on, 'For he's a jolly

good fellow, for he's a jolly good fellow, for he's a jolly good fe-e-llow, who Judas will deny,' in honour of Jesus' birthday.

Then we got down to business. Revengers wanted to know if I'd gone mad. They said that throwing all my Christmas presents away just before Christmas pointed to BIG insanity.

'You should demand the cost of those presents back from Mel and William,' said Ralph.

But I knew they'd never give it to me, so I said, 'Can't be bothered,' like I couldn't be bothered, and, 'I've still got £74.26 in the bank,' like I still had £74.26 in the bank, which, as it happened, I did.

'That's not the point,' said Aaron. 'They opened your presents. They must pay!' He did have a point.

I was miserable as I walked home past Santa's Grotto, past queues of damp and screaming kids. Told Revengers what a lousy Christmas I was expecting, what with the presents disaster, the unacceptable goose and the intrusion of *Hello!* magazine. At the mention of *Hello!*, Aaron and Ralph fell to their knees and tore at my trousers. They

begged me to let them be in the photos too, but I told them no. *Hello!* operates a seeding system, a bit like Wimbledon, which means that the scum of society can't get in. It's all done on the veracity of the father's seed, apparently, and Ralph and Aaron weren't made with my father's seed, so that's them out of the picture.

'It's like that film on telly last night,' said Ralph. '*Six Cents!* with Bruce Willis. He played a father who lost his son because it wasn't his seed that made him.'

'Oh no!' I said. 'I knew there was something I meant to watch last night. I was wrecking my presents instead.' That's the problem with personal crises at Christmas. Not only do they muck up your head, but they muck up your telly schedule as well.

Bad *Things* ⟶ *Things* *Things* ⟶ Worse

William and Mel would not give me their money.

'We've spent it all on our presents,' Mel said.

'If I had any left I'd let you have it,' said Will. This was a surprise. Will never gave me something for nothing, unless it was a clip round the ear. 'To be honest, I feel bad about what we did last night,' he said. 'It's Christmas. We shouldn't be fighting. We should be loving each other. Look, I can't give you money, but I can give you some red-hot advice. Interested?'

'I guess so,' I said.

'Have you told Mum and Dad what you want for Christmas yet?' I hadn't. 'Good,' he said. 'And how much have you got in your bank account?'

'Why should I tell you?' I said.

'Because you've got a choice,' he said. 'It

can either sit there doing you no good or you can turn it into everlasting happiness!'

'Seventy-four pounds,' I told him.

'That's perfect,' he said, 'because it only costs seventy pounds.'

'What does?' The conversation was leaping ahead faster than I could keep up.

'Your present,' he said. 'I mean, you know what you want, don't you?'

'Of course,' I said. 'I was going to ask Father Christmas for a Game Boy Deluxe.'

'A Game Boy Deluxe? Oh no. Really? I don't believe it. What a shame,' he said. 'No, you can't have that. I want that.'

'Do you?' I said. 'That's the first I've heard of it.'

'Think again,' he said.

'OK,' I said. 'I want a mini-disc player.'

'Now, that is a good idea,' said Will, patting me on the shoulder. 'But I'm afraid I've just bagsied that too, so

you'll have to think-again again.'

'Why can't you think-again again?' I said. 'You're the one nicking all my ideas.'

'Because I already know what you want!' he said. 'Alice, I know you better than you know yourself. I'm saving you from inferior gifts so you can have the mother of all presents!'

'My name is Alistair,' I said, 'unless you can see boobs where I can't.'

'Oh, forget it,' said William, standing up and walking to the door. 'How can I do you a favour when you're so ungrateful? You're obviously too young and immature for this present.'

'Too young for what?' I said. 'I'm not! What is it?'

William sat down again. He sighed and looked tired, like he wanted me to think he'd been doing some Einstein-type think-ing on my behalf. 'Remember that lovely pool table you wanted?' he said.

'No,' I said.

'The pool table you wanted. You said so in the summer. You want it. You do.'

'Do I?'

'Yeah – you'll love pool,' he said.

Somehow, and I don't know how, William persuaded me to part with £70 to buy the pool table immediately.

'Why can't I let Mum and Dad pay for it?' I moaned. 'After all, it's their present to me.'

'For the last time,' said Will wearily, like he was explain-ing chess to a gadfly, 'if you don't buy the exact pool table you want now, Mum and Dad will buy the wrong one – that's the cheaper one – tomorrow. You know they will. All parents are cheapskates. So don't

right... ok... so tell me again, what do the prawns do?...

let it happen! Go out, buy the right table yourself, then give the bill to Mum and Dad. They'll love you for it. You'll have done all the hard work for them. No late-night shopping on Christmas Eve. No crowds. Just seventy pounds in cash in your hand. Problem sorted! Bosh!'

'It sounds too complicated to work,' I said.

'Welcome to the grown-up world,' said Will. 'You're protecting your own interests, little brother. You're ensuring Total Present Satisfaction.' And with that he steered me down the stairs and out through the front door. 'I'm coming with you,' he said. 'You obviously can't be trusted.'

Will took me down the road to the bank, stood next to me while I withdrew my money, shoved me into the sports shop, bought the pool table and helped me carry it home. I liked the green one, but he said that blue was much better. He also said that we should open it immediately and start playing.

'But what will I get given on Christmas Day?' I said. 'I won't have a present to open.'

'But you've got it now,' said Will. 'How clever is that? You're a flaming genius!'

So we played pool. Or rather, Will's mates came round and played pool, while I sat on the edge of my bed and watched. 'Can't I have the next game?' I said.

'Of course you can,' said Will, 'if you want to break the table. Look, I'll say it again, Alice. You're a beginner. Everyone knows that a pool table has to settle after being moved, and that is the worst possible time for a beginner to play. You might break it, or "drain" it, as the professionals say. If you drain the

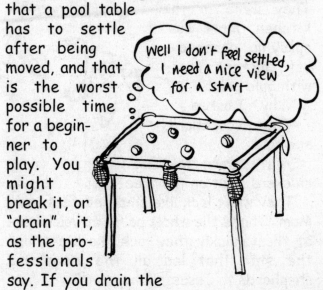

Well I don't feel settled, I need a nice view for a start

slate without the proper filters, the whole pool structure can become very unstable. You end up with what is known as an "empty" pool table, which means you're way down on bounce-back and kissing's like playing Russian roulette. So yeah, you can play if you want to, but you'd be a donkey if you did!'

Bearing all that in mind, I thought I wouldn't play pool just yet. So went off to get my money back from Mum and Dad.

They were in the kitchen. Mum was spraying chopped-off chickens' feet with gold paint.

'Why?' I asked.

'Tree decorations,' she said.

'You're going to hang chickens' feet on the tree?'

'They won't look like chickens' feet,' said Mum. 'That's the whole point. If you glance at them quickly they look like stars, like the star that led all the kings and shepherds to Jesus.'

Mum definitely missed her vocation. She should have been a presenter on *Blue Peter* and *Crimewatch,* specializing in 'making interesting things from unwanted body parts'.

Dad was lying on his stomach on the floor. He had two packets of frozen peas on his back to freeze-dry the pain and was reading a brochure about collagen injections. It showed him how surgeons inject this plastic stuff into the bags under men's eyes to make them look younger. Dad was studying the ingredients in a tube of toothpaste and wondering if he could do it himself with an icing piper.

I told my parents that I wanted a pool table for my Christmas present.

'Oh good!' said Mum. 'Aren't we clever, Daddy?'

But when I told them that I'd already paid for it and wanted my money back now, their faces drained of colour.

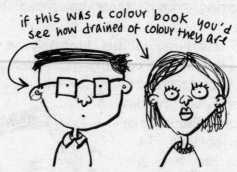

if this WAS a colour book you'd see how drained of colour they are

'But we've already bought you a present,' said Dad. That meant no.

I ran back to my room, but William had invited so many mates round to play pool that I couldn't get in. I rang his mobile and shouted at him down the phone. 'Mum and Dad won't pay!' I said. 'I've lost my money and it's all your fault. It's you who likes pool, not me.'

'Then why did you buy the table?' said William. 'I only suggested, Alice. I didn't force you.'

'You and your mates get out of my room!' I shouted. 'Or I'll ring up Who Wants to Be a Millionaire? and get you on so everyone can see what a thick pig you really are!'

I didn't actually feel like crying, but I thought it was appropriate. To get the tears flowing I thought about dead puppies...

'But I'm not, am I?' said William. 'I'm not the one who's just spent seventy pounds on a pool table I don't even know how to use!' Then my bedroom door opened and William and his friends filed out.

'It's not fair,' I said. 'It was your idea. You've got to give me my money back.'

'But I can't,' said William. 'I've spent all mine on Christmas presents. Didn't I tell you? I've got really brilliant ones this year with Mel.'

STOP MESSING WITH MY CHRISTMAS!

No presents. No money to buy presents. No decorations. No stuffing. No turkey. No Christmas!

I was just starting to cry, when the door barged open and William bounced back in with an armful of presents. 'I thought you might like to see the fabulous presents Mel and I have bought,' he said smugly.

Emergency! Emergency! Emergency!

'Out!' I replied.

But the more I told William to leave the more he stayed, flaunting his and Mel's presents under my nose. Their big joint-presents from both of them and not from me. Their big Goody Two-shoes presents, already wrapped and labelled. Their big lovely presents that were going to look so generous round the tree and make Mum and Dad love them even more than me!

'And you haven't got anyone anything!' smugged-up William. 'Don't you think that's pretty mean?'

I needed money quick. I wasn't having *Hello!* magazine taking photos of me not giving any presents. I'd be branded **THE MEANEST BOY IN BRITAIN** by the tabloids. Small children would make money-rustling noises behind my back. People would sneer at me in the street and call me Scrooge!

THE DAILY DIRT

Fury at the meanest most Scrooge-like boy this side of Shanghai

I phoned Ralph and sang our secret password: 'For he's a jolly good fellow, for he's a jolly good fellow, for he's a jolly good fe-e-llow, who Judas will deny.'

'Who is?' said Ralph's dad.

'Oh, hello, Reverend Ming. Is Ralph in?'

'Who's a jolly good fellow, Alistair?'

'Jesus,' I said. 'It's his birthday.'

'Are you trying to be funny?' he hissed.

'No,' I replied, as the phone went down. I don't think Ralph's dad likes me. Mind you, that comes as no surprise. Vicars are supposed to be nice and holy, but underneath they must be full of anger. This is because only old people go to church these days, and when all the old people die the vicars will be out of a job.

OUT OF WORK

COUNCIL RE CYCLING BINS

PAPER

BOTTLES

CANS

DOG COLLARS

Found Ralph at Aaron's, but they couldn't lend me money either, because they'd spent all theirs on presents too. So went round to Granny Constance's house. She had a sign on her front door written in red felt pen and decorated round the edges with gold glitter. It said,

I have been abandoned by my family this festive season. therefore christmas will not be celebrated at this house. do not bother bringing me meals on wheels or singing your carols. you won't get any money out of me.

I rang the bell several times before Granny heard it over the racing commentary on her telly. 'What do you want?' she said.

'Hello, Granny,' I said. 'Got any jobs you want doing? I won't charge much. It's just so I can buy you a Christmas present.'

'I'm not coming to you for Christmas,' she said. 'I wasn't invited so I'm boating up the Nile, as you very well know. That means I won't be needing a present, which means

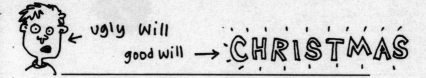

you won't be needing money. Besides which, Alistair, this is the season of goodwill to all men – or hadn't you noticed? – so you should be doing my jobs for free.'

'But I haven't got any presents,' I said. 'I didn't know how else to get them.'

'Make them,' she said. 'In the olden days we could make a computer from a cotton reel. All you need's a little imagination!'

I told her that making presents wasn't what boys did nowadays. 'It's a bit baby-ish,' I said. 'Besides, the last thing I made was at nursery school, and people won't want painted wood shavings or pasta pictures any more. Would you?'

'Certainly not,' she said. 'The ones you gave me then are still cluttering up the attic. If I still had my good legs and a half-decent hip I'd be up there like a shot. I'd chuck them out and burn them!'

49

Aren't Grannies Lovely?

If I could spell youthanazier I might take more of an interest in it.

By the time I got home I'd hatched a plan. I locked William out of the pool hall and sat down on my bed with pen and paper.

Alistair Fury
47 Atrocity Road,
Tooting,
England
(near Argos)
December 19th

TO: Father Christmas, North Pole

Dear Father Christmas,
I'll keep this brief. Hello. How are you? How are the reindeer? How are the elves? How is your red costume? I've been very good this year, apart from blowing up that frog with a bicycle pump, but that was an accident. Someone had nicked the tyre while I wasn't looking and stuck the frog on instead. I suspect William. Which brings

me to the point of this letter. Christmas is my favourite day of the year, as you well know. This year I was ready for it on December 1st. I'd bought my presents, decorated my room and sent my cards. But yesterday my world collapsed. My horrid big brother and sister opened my presents and told everyone what I'd got them. As if that wasn't bad enough, the presents got broken, then they stole my money so I couldn't buy any more, and wouldn't give me their money to make up for it, and nor would Granny, and to top it all William made me buy myself a present I HATE! This is the truth regardless of what my big brother and sister might write in their letters. Now, you would think that I would want REVENGE. Any normal human being would, but not me. All I ask is that you bring me four extra presents on Christmas Eve. One for Dad, one for Mum, one for Mel and one for William, because <u>Hello!</u> are here and I can't look mean.

See you (or rather <u>won't</u> see you!) on Christmas Eve. Good luck. Sleigh them dead!
Love,
Alistair

Doorbell rang several times while I was addressing the envelope. Just in case it was a really big surprise present for me, I left letter on bed and ran downstairs. Melanie was standing in the hall next to the front door, having just come back from work. The bell rang again. She ignored it and carried on checking her spots for make-up.

'Why can't you answer it?' I said. But being so grown up, she wasn't talking to me for telling Gabriel her real age. So she stomped upstairs and I opened the door.

'Dustmen,' said one of the three men outside. 'Happy Christmas.'

'Thank you,' I said. 'And Happy Christmas to you too.'

But as I went to shut the door the biggest man put his foot in it. 'You don't under- stand,' he said. 'Even though we're obviously not ask- ing for money, we're collecting for our Christmas box.'

I gave them a hinge and three screws from the cellar. 'No wood,' I said. 'Sorry.'

I have never heard of a Christmas box before. It's probably for keeping Christmas cigars in, or burying hamsters that don't make it through the festive season.

Or maybe dustmen play cricket on Christmas Day.

PREPARE TO BE HORRIFIED LIFE-CRUSHING SHOCK COMING UP!

Went back to bedroom to find William and Mel reading my letter to Father

Christmas. Both of them were in hysterics. They could hardly talk.

'What's so funny?' I shouted.

'You!' William pointed.

Mel screamed and flopped all over him. 'You really believe he exists, don't you?' she said.

'Who?'

'Father Christmas.'

'Of course he does,' I told her. 'How else would our presents get here, Dumbo?'

'Oh my God!' wheezed William weakly. 'I can't believe we're telling you this.'

'Telling me what?' I yelled. I didn't know what they were on about.

'Father Christmas isn't real,' said Mel. 'It's Mum and Dad.'

I felt like someone had injected ice into my veins. Like suddenly I was floating outside my body watching my mouth open and close like a goldfish. Then all of a sudden the noise of my big brother and sister's laughter roared through my head like a high-speed train and I rushed out of the room.

The peas had thawed so Dad was lying under packets of frozen scampi. Mum was spray-painting a dead bird that Napoleon

had dragged through the cat-flap. And I was not making any sense.

'What are you saying?' repeated my dad.

'That Will and Mel say Father Christmas doesn't exist,' I said.

'Oh blimey,' chuckled my dad. 'Well, I

hate to tell you this, Alistair, but he—'

'Does,' said my mum. 'Don't listen to them, Alistair. They all think they're so grown up, but underneath they're not.'

'So he does or doesn't exist?' I said. 'I'm confused.'

So were my parents, because Mum said, 'Does,' and Dad said nothing because Mum was treading on his fingers.

'Better now?' said Mum.

'I don't know,' I said. 'I feel numb. What are you doing?'

Mum was sewing up the bird's bottom. 'I'm going to put it on top of the tree instead of that horrible fairy,' she said.

'But we always have that horrible fairy,' I said.

'Not this year, Alistair. This year, I thought we'd have a little Christmas robin for *Hello!*'

'It's a starling,' I said.

'That's why I'm painting it red,' she said.

'But it's dead,' I said. 'It'll decompose.'

'No it won't,' she said. 'We've stuffed it with toothpaste.'

'I want to see how toothpaste performs under household conditions,' said Dad, fingering his eye bags. 'It'll be a lot cheaper than collagen if it sets. You've seen the way it hardens round the edges of the tube.'

well at least my breath won't smell

'It's sweet, isn't it?' said Mum. 'After people have seen it perching in Hello! I bet toothpaste birds will be all the rage next year.'

STOP MESSING WITH MY CHRISTMAS!

Has my family gone completely mad? Is there no Christmas tradition that they don't want to change?

'For he's a jolly good fellow, for he's a jolly good fellow, for he's a jolly good fe-e-llow, who Judas will deny.'

'Not you again,' hissed the voice at the other end of the phone.

'Sorry, Reverend Ming. Can I speak to Ralph, please?'

There were muffled voices, then, 'What do you want?' said Ralph. 'You keep upsetting my dad, and every time he gets upset he turns the telly off!'

'Ralph,' I said. 'That's not important any more. The world's just gone topsy-turvy. We've got to meet, mate. There's something I've got to tell you and it's not good news. So bring a mattress to faint onto, all right? See you tomorrow morning at Toss-Bros.'

20.35 Phoned Aaron, then went straight to bed. Didn't want to see my family again that night. They had betrayed me. If it was true what William and Mel had told me, then Mum and Dad had LIED to me for eleven long years!

Too depressed to watch telly.

22.25 Can't sleep. Keep having same horrid dream about Father Christmas.

MY SAME HORRID DREAM THAT I KEEP HAVING ABOUT FATHER CHRISTMAS

It is snowing and I am running hand in hand with a chubby snowman towards a magic sleigh pulled by eight smiling reindeer. Sitting in the sleigh is Father Christmas surrounded by tons of presents, mainly Game Boy Deluxes and mini-disc players. He waves to me and I hear him call.

'Bye-bye, Alistair Fury. You were the last child on earth to know the truth, and now that you have lost your innocence I shall be off.' Then he takes off into the sky and flies straight into the middle of a flock of migrating geese. He just disappears. And when he comes out the other side they've eaten him. His sleigh's still there, but Father Christmas and his faithful reindeer are just skeletons.

I hate geese.

TV MISSED
BBC2, 10.15: Snothunters
Many-mini-movie Channel, 13.15:
Brownie Badge of Honour
C4, 16.00: Dr Soulfighter and the Curse of
Dragon's Rock
BBC1, 19.00 This Is Your Lie
ITV, 19.30: Who's Been Maimed?
ITV, 20.00: Wham! Bam! Crash! Police
Accident!
C5, 22.30: Ibiza Eater

DECEMBER 20

5 days to Christmas

TODAY'S TV
C4, 9.00: The Big Banana
Style Channel, 13.00: Cooking with Chinchillas
BBC1, 15.00: House in a Mess
BBC2, 17.30: The Naked Policeman
C5, 19.30: Knee Tremblers
MTV, 23.00: Dr Wolf's Wild and Wacky Wecord World

More devastating developments. Had to eat breakfast standing up, because Mum had stacked boxes of decorations on the kitchen table and Dad has orders not to come home without a Christmas tree. I HATE decorating the tree – I always get the climbing jobs. Being the smallest, I'm always the one who has to shin up the trunk to reach the dangerous branches at the top. When I come down I've got so many pine needles stuck in me that I look like I've got hairy legs. Every year I complain, and every year the family calls me Squirrel Boy, and William tells me to get up there sharpish or he'll squash my nuts! Nice.

Plus, when I was four I caused an accident. I thought the tree was the Matterhorn and tried to climb it wearing William's football boots for grip. Unfortunately the tree toppled over under my weight and smashed all Mum's expensive ornaments. Since then, it has been a family sport at Christmas to tease me to tears about the damage I caused. After seven years the joke has worn thin.

Stuffed starling/robin dried on boiler overnight and is standing on its own. Maybe toothpaste has life-giving powers as well and the dead bird will shortly fly away. Sniffed beak. Still does not smell dead. Its breath smells of spearmint, which is much nicer.

Left to meet Revengers. Met angry Mel standing by a puddle outside the house.

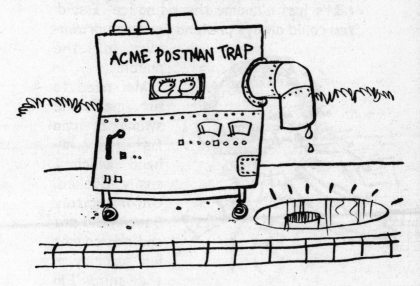

Last night she poured a bucket of water over the pavement, hoping it would freeze by this morning. It was still a puddle.

'I know why you wanted that puddle to freeze,' I said. 'So that when Gabriel comes round the corner – stop me if I'm getting warm, Melanie – you can pretend to slip and fall at his feet. Then you can look up his trousers – I mean, then you can groan like a damsel in distress and he can be your shining knight and save you.'

'Go away!' she hissed. 'I'm not talking to you.'

'It's just a shame there's no ice,' I said. 'You could always pretend you were drowning in the puddle!'

Mel tried to hit me. She swung a limp fist at my head, which I easily ducked. Unfortunately Gabriel did not and she caught him squarely on the chin. 'I'm sorry,' she squeaked, bursting into tears. 'It was that horrible verminous orphan child again! Why, oh why, oh why was he not strangled at birth!' I think Mel is confusing being a grown-up with being a Nazi.

Father Christmas's costume was drying by an open window outside the Toss-Bros-Snoss-Gross loo. Both trouser legs were stained above the knee. The sight of it brought back painful memories from last

night's dream. I walked past it with my head bowed. I was still grieving for the late FC.

Aaron and Ralph were eager to hear my earth-shattering news.

'Father Christmas doesn't exist!' snorted Aaron. 'Is that all? We've known that for years. Everyone knows that.'

'So who drinks the beer and eats the mince pies?' I said.

'Mum and Dad,' said Ralph.

'Your mum and dad eat my mince pies?'

'No, your mum and dad!' said Ralph.

'But how do they squeeze down the chimney?'

'They don't have to. They hide the

presents in the house and sneak them into your stocking on Christmas Eve.'

'And in case the midwife hit you extra hard with the Stupid Stick, that is not Father Christmas in the Grotto,' said Aaron. 'That's Mr Cloutman the ironmonger.'

I wondered why all the kids were going home with hacksaws and screwdrivers.

I didn't want to cry – I mean, it seemed such a cissy thing to cry about – but I felt like I'd just lost a friend. I howled and wailed and snorted snot in great big juddering waves. There was a banging on the door and a voice shouted out.

His mind was as empty as my bank account.

'Security. Are you all right in there?'

'Yes, thanks,' said Ralph, trying to make his voice sound older. 'See the OUT OF ORDER sign on the door? We're just fixing the . . . erm . . . just fixing the . . . erm . . . Anyway, my mate just whacked the ball-cock with a hammer by mistake.'

'Oof! Painful,' said security.

'Yeah. It's as big as a beach ball now,' said Ralph.

'All right,' I hissed. 'Don't overdo it!'

When security had gone, Aaron asked me if I was all right?

I told him I was. 'Mind you,' I said, 'if this is growing up I want to stop now!'

There was a big score to settle. My family had trashed my childhood and wrecked my Christmas in more ways than one. Five to be precise. No Father Christmas, no turkey, no presents, no money to buy presents and a pool table I didn't want. Yesterday, I was an innocent flower, a pure white snowdrop, untouched by the manure of adult lies. Today, I am a sewage pipe!

We put our heads together and came up with some Xmas revenges.

A MODERN CAROL
FOR CHRISTMAS
The Xmas Trojan Donkey

Little Donkey, Little Donkey
On the dusty way.
Got revenges
In your insides
With which to make my family pay!

Revenge for Mum

For Mum, the Turkey Traitor, it is
Operation Goose Bump! The aim is to re-
instate turkey as the centrepiece of
Christmas lunch and pay back Mum at the
same time for daring to fiddle with the
menu. We felt like medieval earls and
dukes planning to depose the evil goose

from the throne and replace it with the rightful king – King Turkey XI!

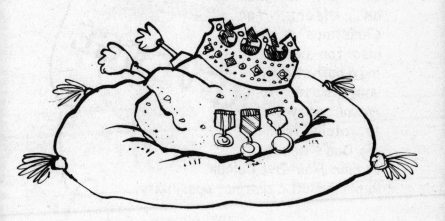

Got the idea for the revenge from the over-gummed pig's trotter in the front garden. The idea is to creep into the kitchen every night and chuck one item of food into the garden, so that in the morning everyone will think we've had a fox in the kitchen. So then when I finally chuck away the goose they won't blame me. They'll blame the fox. And if I chuck away the goose close enough to Christmas Day Mum won't have time to buy another, so we'll have to have turkey!

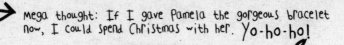
mega thought: If I gave Pamela the gorgeous bracelet now, I could spend Christmas with her. Yo-ho-ho!

Revenge for Dad

For not doing the normal stuffing and generally not making an effort for Christmas and also for becom- ing a pathetically vain slave to *Hello!*, we voted to totally tram- ple Dad's beauty regime. Hair-Dye Colour Replacement a distinct possibility!

Revenge for the Evil Twins of Destruction

For William and Mel I reserved my most horri- ble revenges! We all agreed that teasing Mel about Gabriel was good for getting under her skin on a daily basis, and that playing William at pool for money and BEATING! him like a SKUNK-BREATHED BABY! would bring us all more joy than <u>even</u> one of Pamela Whitby's smiles.

Aaron pointed out that for me to beat William at pool I would need to practise and improve my game. Ralph laughed involuntarily. When I prove my doubters wrong I shall expect a profuse apology and gallons of grovelling.

But for the main course of revenge this is what we chose:

'They wrecked my presents,' I said, 'so I wreck theirs. It's tit for tat. A tie for a tie! A hoof for a hoof!'

We're going to embarrass them to Hell in front of *Hello!*,* by swapping their real presents – the ones they showed me last night – for really rude stuff wrapped up in similar boxes and paper. Then, on Christmas Day, William and Mel will look like sick perverts for giving such scummy presents!

'But we can't do that,' said Ralph. 'We haven't got any money, so we can't buy any rude and embarrassing presents until we've sold the real ones.'

'And Mel and William will notice if their real presents go missing,' said Aaron.

It became a two-part plan. First, we had to steal the real presents and replace them with empty boxes of

71

similar size and wrapping paper. Second, after selling the real presents and buying the really rude presents, we had to swap the empty wrapped boxes for new wrapped boxes containing the really rude stuff. Sorted!

'It'd be simpler to assassinate them,' said Ralph.

'I know,' I said. 'But I'm not allowed.'

Aaron was desperate to know what really rude presents we had in mind.

'Fake vomit,' I said, 'plastic doggy-do's, that funny apron with the big boobs, condoms . . .'

'But won't we have to go into shops and buy them?' he said.

'Of course we will!' I said.

That was the bit he was scared of. Last time he'd tried to buy condoms, the cashier had held them up in front of a huge queue of women and girls, and shouted, 'Condoms! Eensy-weensy cockroach size. Do we do them half price for children?'

'I nearly died,' said Aaron.

Suddenly the door to the Toss-Bros-Snoss-Gross loo opened and Father Christmas came in. There was an embarrassed silence while he stood at the urinal and we stood behind him, trying to look like we were doing something other than staring.

The silence was obviously too much for him. 'Yo ho ho!' he said. 'And what do you three boys want for Christmas?'

It seemed a bit rude saying, 'Why should we tell you, Mr Cloutman?' So instead I mumbled, 'Game Boy Deluxe,' while the others looked at me like I was mad.

Then Father Christmas washed his hands, dried them on his beard and left. A tiny little part of me secretly hoped that everyone else was wrong and Mr Cloutman was in fact the real Father Christmas just having a laugh by pretending to be an ironmonger.

'By the way,' said Ralph. 'Did you see *Who's Been Maimed?* last night, Alistair? It was brilliant.'

Of course I hadn't seen *Who's Been Maimed?* I hadn't been near a television set for TWO days! Call this Christmas? It was more like prison!

Dad came home with the littlest tree you ever saw. Sell-by date of 1998 on the label. Mum went off her trolley and asked him what he thought Hello! would make of such a needleless specimen.

MUM →

MUM's trolley →

'I ran out of money,' Dad said. 'Had to buy these in the chemist.'

'These' were a jumbo bottle of spray-on tan and a box of black hair-dye, which were essential, he said, for bringing him fame and fortune. He has big plans for the money he's going to make from modelling. No more leisure centre manager for him. In a year's time he's going to have his own chain of leisure centres called 'Fudge and Fury', specializing in keep-fit and cream cakes to attract figure-conscious fatties. He was sent back to get a proper tree, but not before he'd lathered himself in fake tan first.

Mel was too grown up to help decorate the new tree. Her scabby, pus-infected nose-ring hole needed poking out and swabbing. William was too busy playing pool in my bedroom and Dad was taking a bath in the tanning lotion, which was strictly forbidden on the bottle.

'Something will go wrong,' said Mum.

But Dad was happy to take the risk if it meant he looked like a Greek god in the photos.

So it was just Mum and me decorating the tree, which meant that it took hours and hours and hours and hours, and drove a bulldozer through my TV schedule. I thought the chickens' feet looked exactly like chickens' feet, but Mum thought they twinkled. She thought the stuffed starling/robin looked much better than the horrible fairy, but I thought it looked ghoulish. It seemed to have a white tapeworm hanging from its bottom and its eyes followed me around the hall, like it was blaming me for turning it into a toothpaste-dispenser!*

Finally we nailed the funeral wreath to the front door and hung the mistletoe over the bottom of the stairs on a piece of red ribbon.

'Mel,' I shouted, 'we've got the mistletoe up so you can suffocate Gabriel with a full-face snog tomorrow!' She flicked a dirty piece of cotton wool with a plug of something smelly on it into my hair. 'Love you too!' I shouted, while my mind ran round in circles chasing its tail at the thought of kissing. Wouldn't it be wonderful if when I give Pamela Whitby her Christmas bracelet – which I keep on me at all times in case I get a chance to surprise her – she wanted to kiss me under the mistletoe! Have snapped off small twig and put in pocket just in case.

Then Mum did the annual joke: 'Now, don't go climbing that tree and knocking all the ornaments off, will you, Alistair? I know what you're like.'

'I was four, Mum.'

After which, all the presents were stacked around the tree and it suddenly felt a lot more Christmassy. Or at least it would have done had there been any presents for me.

'Our one won't fit under the tree,' winked Mum.

So Mum and Dad were forgiven, but my big brother and sister hadn't even bought me one present between them.

'Why should we buy you a present if you don't buy one for us?' said William.

'But I did!' I said. 'You opened them.'

'Yes,' said William, 'but you tore them up!'

This was the final straw.

A CRIME AGAINST CHRISTMAS!

NOT buying me a present was a crime against Christmas and crime deserves punishment. Hard labour would be good, or hanging. But can't find judge who'll do it for me. Yellow Pages were useless. Looked under 'Judge', 'Rock-breaking' and 'Death Sentence' – nothing under any of them.

I phone Revengers and told them it was on for midnight, then I slipped into the night to find myself some cardboard boxes.

'Where are you going?' Mum shouted after me, as I ran down the street.

'Carol singing,' I shouted back. 'Carol singing!'

Hark, the Herald Angels Sing, Mel and Will will be done in!

Instead of spending the evening watching lovely television, I spent it wrapping empty cardboard boxes. Some people think that there's more entertainment in a cardboard box than there is on television, but I think those people should be smote down with a fiery axe for such blasphemy. Christmas TV is my religion.

22.15 Finished wrapping. Tried pool. Cannot work out why cue has got a big rubber doorstop on the end. When I hit the white ball with it, it just bounces off in all directions.

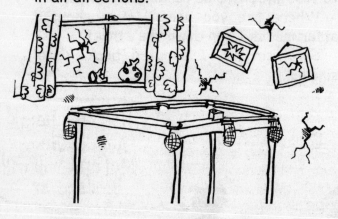

23.55 Everyone asleep when I crept downstairs on my double mission. First I opened the kitchen window and chucked six eggs into the bushes.

'Oi!' came a shout from the darkness. 'What are you doing?'

'You just splatted my hair!' whined a second voice.

It was Ralph and Aaron, who were lurking in the shadows waiting to collect the presents as part of Mission Two.

'Sorry,' I whispered. 'That was Operation Goose Bump! Presents next.'

Then I nicked William and Mel's presents from under the tree, opened the front door and chucked them out into Ralph and Aaron's arms – only because of the slimy egg on their fingers some of the presents slipped through and smashed on the gravel.

'Ssssh!' I hissed. 'You'll wake someone up. See you in the morning.'

Then, while Ralph and Aaron scarpered with the booty, I fetched the newly wrapped empty boxes from upstairs and left them under the tree. It looked like nothing had been touched. So far so good.

00.05 On the way back to bed, however, Mr E – he of the acid pee – approached the tree, cocked his leg and let forth a stream of steaming death. As the branches visibly wilted, I gaped in horror. But that was not

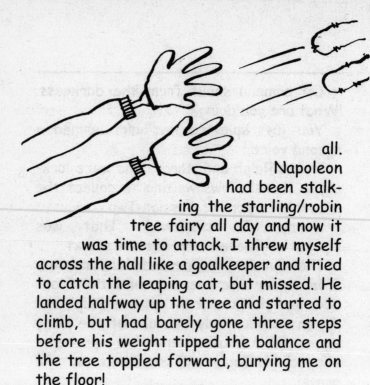

all.
Napoleon had been stalking the starling/robin tree fairy all day and now it was time to attack. I threw myself across the hall like a goalkeeper and tried to catch the leaping cat, but missed. He landed halfway up the tree and started to climb, but had barely gone three steps before his weight tipped the balance and the tree toppled forward, burying me on the floor!

Goes without saying that the whole family woke up and blamed me for climbing the tree like I'd done when I was four.

'Once a tree vandal always a tree vandal,' said William smugly.

I protested my innocence and blamed the pets, but nobody believed me. I was condemned without trial.

'Perhaps Alice needs psychiatric help,' said Melanie. 'Maybe he's got a fear of trees.'

'I'll give you a fear of trees,' I said,

picking up a broken branch and flicking her bum with it. Dad sent me to my bedroom while William and Mel snickered behind my back like serpents.

Mum was crying. She was crouched on the floor mourning her stuffed starling/robin, which had split on impact with the carpet. Mr E was licking up the puddle of runny toothpaste. I stopped on the stairs. Maybe if I said something loving and consoling, my family would forgive me.

'At least Mr E won't have breath like a cow's fart for once!' I said. I don't think that was quite loving enough.

TV MISSED
C4, 9.00: The Big Banana
Style Channel, 13.00: Cooking with Chinchillas
BBC1, 15.00: House in a Mess
BBC2, 17.30: The Naked Policeman
C5, 19.30: Knee Tremblers
MTV, 23.00: Dr Wolf's Wild and Wacky Wecord World

DECEMBER 21
4 days to Christmas

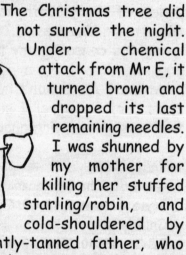

The Christmas tree did not survive the night. Under chemical attack from Mr E, it turned brown and dropped its last remaining needles. I was shunned by my mother for killing her stuffed starling/robin, and cold-shouldered by my lightly-tanned father, who now had to go out and buy another tree. He was enjoying Christmas even less than I was.

When the missing eggs were spotted in the garden, I tried to act surprised. I didn't want to raise suspicions, so I didn't say, 'I bet it was a fox,' right away. I

worked my way subtly towards it.

'What do you think it could have been?' I
said. 'A mongoose?'

'A mongoose?' said Mum. 'In Tooting?'

'An eagle then? Or a python? Ooh! How
about a shark?'

'It was you, wasn't it?' said Dad.

'No it wasn't!' I cried, trying to climb out
of the hole I'd just dug for myself. 'Sharks
eat eggs. Turtles' eggs!'

'No, they don't,' said William. 'Turtles
bury their eggs in sand. Which particular
species of shark
can crawl up a
beach?'

'Man-eating
sharks,' I said. 'It's
well known that you
are what you eat,
so they must be
half man. That
means they can
hold their breath,
thicko!'

'I wish you'd hold your breath!' said Mel,
leaping up from the table. She'd just
spotted Gabriel coming towards our house.
'Bye!' she shouted, running to open the

front door so she could bump into him by chance. But when she opened the door, Gabriel was nowhere to be seen. My note on the funeral wreath had done the trick!

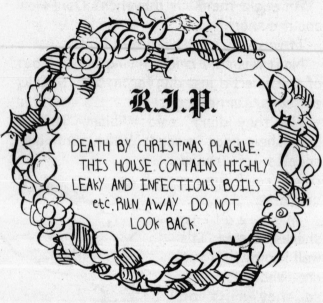

Apart from the presents we'd stolen from Will and Mel, Ralph garden shed was full of old dog collars, used-up candles and broken religious statues. Ralph's reverend dad was saving them up for a graveyard sale. That's like a garage sale only run by the church. Apparently, churches don't have garages, because vicars use bikes instead of cars.

We assumed that selling Will and Mel's presents to make money to buy some really rude stuff would be easy. That was before we discovered what had happened during the midnight window drop. Mum's kitchen clock was broken. Dad's abdominizer was dented. Granny's boxed set of miniature china warthogs was smashed. Mel's pot pourri from William was split. Only William's aftershave from Mel was still in one piece, but it stank of unwashed goat!

I was still upset that Mel and William hadn't bought anything for me.

'They didn't have to give you much, did they?' said Aaron supportively. 'A chocolate orange would have been enough.'

'No it wouldn't,' I said. 'A chocolate orange is disgusting. It's what you give a nearly-dead-aunt you really hate.'

'Oh,' said Aaron quietly.

'Aaron's bought everyone he knows a chocolate orange this year,' said Ralph. There was a long embarrassed silence. Then Ralph coughed. 'Did anyone see *The Naked Policeman* last night?' he asked.

'No!' I screamed. We dropped that topic of conversation too.

Because most of the presents were

broken we figured our best chance of selling them was to flog them to old
shopkeepers with bad eyesight. So we
went to Oxfam. But the three old ladies
behind the counter were unimpressed by
our demand for £50.

'These miniature china warthogs are
broken,' said one.

'Not broken,' lied Ralph. 'Their heads
come off because they're lids. They're
tiny little pots for keeping useful things
in. Like a paper clip or one coffee bean or
a toenail.'

'No thank you,' she said.

'And does this clock work?' asked the
second old lady.

'Oh yes,' I said. 'I know it looks like it's

empty (ha ha!)

smashed to smithereens, but that's because it's a kit. You put it together yourself. That's half the fun. That's why so many people want them. That's why they're so expensive.'

'If it's so expensive, why has it stopped?' she asked.

'That's the stopwatch feature,' I said.

'And what's that?' said the third old lady, taking a sniff of William's aftershave. 'Skunk spray?'

It turned out that they were just cruelly playing with us, because Oxfam don't pay for any of their gear. All of it's donated. So we left in high dungeon, but as we were going, the first old lady took pity on us and made us an offer. 'We'll give you fifty p,' she said.

'For the lot?' I said. 'That's daylight robbery!'

'No,' she said. 'Just for the abdominizer.'

'But they cost sixty pounds in the shops!' I protested, trying to get the price up by lying.

'Oh, we don't want to sell it,' she said.

'It's for our gym out the back.'

With the broken presents under our arms we left the Oxfam shop, disgusted at the uncharitable behaviour of the crumbling generation. If we didn't sell these presents our revenge plan was dead in the water. None of us had done street trading before, but Aaron said that he and Ralph would keep watch while I knocked the presents out to passers-by.

'But it's illegal,' I said.

'So's peeing in the public baths, but we all do it, don't we?' said Aaron.

'Do we?' I said.

'No,' said Ralph.
'Oh,' said Aaron. Just him then.

I did my best to sell the bust-up presents, but nobody was interested. In fact, most people crossed the road to avoid my cries of 'Cumagay' and 'Geyacrimapayerear'. Aaron and Ralph were useless lookouts. Every time they saw someone in uniform they got scared and pretended they weren't with me. I knew I was in trouble when they ran away. Seconds later a policewoman grabbed me from behind and took off her hat. I don't know who was more surprised – me or Miss Bird. Miss Bird is my scummy form teacher. All pigeon-nosed and strict and fussy about rules and regulations. In my time at school she has given me more detentions than she's had smiles in her whole life. Now it would appear she's a constable too.

'Fury!' she gasped when she recognized me.

'Hello, Miss Bird,' I said.

She asked me what I was doing there, so I told her, and she said that if I did it any more she'd run me over. Then she confiscated all the presents and told me to vanish.

'So you're not going to send me to prison?' I said.

'If you want to go,' she said, 'I can arrange it.'

'No,' I said. Then, because I couldn't leave without asking, 'Are you not coming back to school then, Miss Bird? Have you given up teaching for policing?'

'Certainly not,' she said. 'I get bored in the school holidays. I miss all those detentions and lines and pointless little jobs I make you do around the school. So I became a part-time special constable.'

'Oh,' I said. 'So you're not a proper policeman?'

She sucked in air and whistled through her teeth. 'I still have handcuffs,' she said.

I ran.

And ran. And didn't stop running till I saw something utterly brilliant on a market stall. It was green hair-dye: 20p

like scrubbing the loos with a toothbrush.!

92

the lot! Perfect for a Papa Payback!

Back home, I poured Dad's black dye down the sink and replaced it in the bottle

with green. What with him being Irish and having green hair, readers of *Hello!* will think he's a leprechaun! Then, in teeny tiny letters no bigger than iron filings, I wrote myself an alibi at the bottom of the label. I wrote it so small Dad would have needed a magnifying glass to read it.

WARNING: If applied while using fake tan your hair might turn green.

I left a note under the bottle of dye. It was poignant, bitter, witty, cutting and steeped in betrayal all at the same time. It said,

Love, Father Christmas

That was Dad paid back for not putting his heart and soul into Christmas!

The second new tree went up in the hall. Mum had saved the decorations that weren't smashed last night and re-dressed it. It didn't look bad considering. A bit threadbare, but better than a poke in the eye with a needleless Christmas tree. To add a bit of colour Mum spray-painted six doughnuts and hung them off the longest branches. I think Mum has got a little bit of tom cat in her. She can't stop spraying!

One of the things that didn't survive was the stuffed starling/robin, so the horrible fairy was unpacked. I'd forgotten how horrible it really was. Basically it was an old Action Man of William's dressed in a fairy frock. He had a scar on his cheek and grenades in his trouser

Oh the shame, if Sindy could see me now

pocket, but under the dress you didn't notice. The problem was wings. He didn't have any. I made some out of two pig's ears that Mum had bought as a treat for Mr E on Christmas Day: sprayed them gold and glued them onto Fairy Man's back.

Again Dad did not help. He had more important things to do, like dyeing his hair and overdosing on fake tan. When he came downstairs Mum and I both burst out laughing at the lump of green turf on the top of his head. It made up for losing the presents!

'Hang on,' I said. 'You remind me of something. Yellow skin. Green top . . . It's a parsnip!'

Dad was not amused. In fact he burst out crying. I told him to stop, because the tears were leaving white streaks down his yellow face, where the fake tan hadn't soaked in yet.

When I pointed out the warning that Dad had 'obviously missed' at the bottom of the bottle, he slumped onto the sofa and hit himself with a cushion. 'How could I have been so stupid!' he said.

'It's the way you were born,' I told him. Then, because he couldn't leave the house, he ordered me to go and buy him some new black hair-dye straight away. He'd read about this industrial-strength stuff called Dye Hard, which was the bee's knees, apparently. I told him I'd do it in the morning. After all, it seemed a shame

to spoil a whole evening of fun, watching Dad fluoresce and glow in the dark!

Told Mum that if we wanted this new tree to last, we'd have to stop Mr E from peeing on it. She came up with the idea of a nappy. Rather inventive, I thought, for a mum. Problem was, she only had old-fashioned nappies. They were made from small beach towels that had to be folded six hundred and twenty-three times. Getting one on Mr E was impossible. He wouldn't stay still long enough. So Mum called William down to help and the three of us wrestled the nappy onto the dog. It was spooky how much he looked like the little baby Jesus in his swaddling clothes. Only uglier, obviously. If Jesus was the Son of God, then Mr E was the Son of Dog!

When Mum left the hall, William thought it was amusing to wrestle a nappy onto me. I wouldn't have minded, but the doorbell rang in the middle and before I could get the safety pin undone he'd opened the front door! There I was, all nappied up, staring at a bunch of carol singers, and most of them were GIRLS! I looked like a miniature sumo wrestler.

The carol singers stopped singing and started giggling, leaving their leader, my wart-ridden piano teacher Mrs Muttley, puffing away on her penny recorder. The high-pitched squeal she made on her instrument was so piercing that Mr E and Napoleon shoved dog food in their ears to blot out the pain. Then everyone crammed into the hall to sing, *just to complete my humiliation*

'We wish you a merry Christmas and a nappy new year!'

and I saw Pamela Whitby. She was lurking at the back. Horror! I tore at the nappy, but it wouldn't come off. William had

locked the safety pin. And when I looked up again, it was all over. Mrs Muttley had got her money off Mum and was herding everyone out so she could sprint down the chippie for a fish supper.

'Pamela,' I called out, pushing through the crowd. She had those disapproving eyes again. 'I've got  something I want to give you.'

She looked at me like I meant hepatitis. Then she glanced up, saw the mistletoe and turned purple. 'I do *not* kiss babies!' she screamed, slapping me hard across the face.

I was stunned. 'No . . .' I cried, feeling for my gift. 'I meant, give you this . . .' But Pamela had melted into the darkness.

'Never mind,' said Mrs Muttley. 'I'll be your Mistletoe Miss if you like, Alistair.' And before I could say no, she had leaned across, grabbed my cheeks with her warty hands and planted a big wet kiss on my lips. 'Sorry about the cold sore,' she said. 'Night!'

Rushed up to my bedroom and washed my mouth with soap and water. Afterwards, practised pool so that I could execute a double-payback on William (re presents and now nappy) by crushing him by five frames to nil and winning all his money. Quickly mastered the art of hitting the white ball. Then moved on to white ball hitting spotted ball. Less success here. Then the phone rang. It was Ralph and Aaron checking to see if I'd been arrested by the policewoman or not.

'Yes,' I said.

'So how come you're at home?' gasped Ralph.

'I killed a prison guard and escaped,' I said. 'They've got bloodhounds on the street. I've just come back for a few things before I disappear ... for ever.' There was a horrified silence down the line. 'No, of course I wasn't arrested. But it was no thanks to you, you creampuffs!'

'We'll make it up to you,' said Ralph. 'Meet in the Toss-Bros-Snoss-Gross loo tomorrow morning. I think I've got another brilliant money-making plan.'

'Good,' I said, 'because I don't think my money-making plan's going to work.'

When I entered William's bedroom, he was digging at his verruca with a teaspoon. It had changed shape. It didn't look like Mr E's bottom any more, it looked like Moby Dick.

'Fancy a game of pool?' I asked. 'We could have a bet on it.'

'Have you been practising?' he said suspiciously.

'Just a bit,' I said.

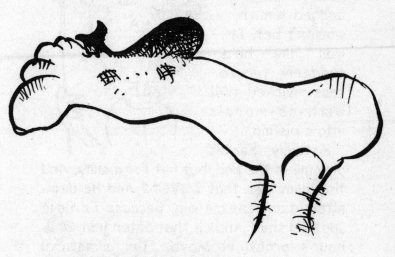

'So you're good?' he said.

'Of course I'm not,' I laughed – when secretly I knew I was better than yesterday.

'That's what all the hustlers say,' said William. 'How much do you want to bet?'

'Seventy pounds,' I said.

'No way. You haven't got it to lose, Alistair. It'd be robbery. I couldn't.' It didn't matter how hard I begged him, he wouldn't bet. It was like he'd suddenly turned from wicked-Will-with-no-morals into a bishop.

Actually, he did play me in the end, but not for money. And the irony was that I WON! And he definitely didn't let me win, because I'd have spotted that. And all that after just ONE hour's practice! Maybe I'm a natural genius and will go on to become one of the game's greats, earning so much money that I can blow my nose on £50 notes!

'You're good,' said William. 'I'm going to

have to watch you, Alistair, or one day you'll have the shirt off my back!'

SHIRT OFF WILL'S BACK

Yeah, I thought, and your trousers, socks, vest and pants!

00.23 Operation Goose Bump – Stage Two. Threw contents of cheeseboard out tonight. Scattered smelly Stilton etc. at bottom of garden in fox-like manner. On the way back in, however, I trod in something that made my blood run cold. Mr E's nappy! The fact that it was lying in the middle of the lawn meant that he wasn't wearing it. I rushed back in to save the tree, but I was too late. Arrived in the hall to find Mr E fully cocked, pointing Pongo at the tree trunk again and sniffing the air like he'd just smelled something good. It was the fairy's wings. The festive pig's ears.

With one podge-mungous leap the porky pug launched himself at the top of the tree, but landed only halfway up. For the second time in two nights he brought the Christmas tree crashing down around my ears.

00.43 Sent back to my bedroom. The noise of the falling tree and the little glass tinkles woke my humourless family for the second night in a row. I explained how I'd heard the fox stealing the cheese and how, when I'd come down to stop him, I'd found him climbing the tree for the pig's ears, but they wouldn't believe me.

'All right, maybe it wasn't a fox,' I said.

'You mean, maybe it was a pig,' said Mum.

'Could be,' I said.

'A deaf pig,' she ranted, 'trying to get his ears back!'

'I wouldn't know if he was earless or not,' I said. 'I didn't get that close a look. It was dark.'

'Don't be such a liar!' she shouted, losing

her temper. 'How could a two-ton pig climb a Christmas tree?'

'Well, maybe it didn't climb,' I said weakly. 'Maybe it flew.'

'If pigs can fly,' shouted Mum, 'then your dad's stupid face doesn't look like a stupid stripy yellow deckchair!'

01.18 Dad's stupid face does look like a stupid stripy yellow deckchair. Does that mean pigs can't fly? If so, I have just wasted half an hour at the window looking for them.

01.32 Must get on top of this telly thing. If I'm not careful I'll go through the whole holiday without seeing a single programme. What sort of suck-ass Christmas would that be?!

TV MISSED
BBC2, 11.30: Living in the Lice Age
Hoorah!, 13.00: Boys and Bicycles
Movie Extra Plus, Plus One More, 15.00: Pin Head's Big Adventure
BBC1, 20.00: The Thickest Link
C5, 21.30: Sex on a Stick

TODAY'S TV
Cartoon Channel, 09.30: Specky Spooks
BBC2, 10.45: Wicked Witches
C4, 11.30: Gnaughty Gnomes
**Really Bad Family Movies Channel,
14.00:** Santa Gets the Sack!
ITV, 19.00: Charlie Chuckle's Celebrity
Cracker
C5, 20.30: Sun, Sand and Shagaluf
Brrrrrm!, 23.00: Cars of the Body Snatchers

07.45 Another tree dead from Mr E's poisoned pee. Mum opened the front door with a long face* and hurled out the brown stump.

'Suppose I'd better go out and get another one,' said Dad, whose face was slowly turning khaki. Then he remembered that he couldn't go out because his hair was green. Mum had to do it.

'Like I do everything else around here,' she hissed. Then she set a mousetrap in the kitchen and went out. Either she was stupid, thinking she could catch a fox with a mousetrap, or she didn't really believe my story about the fox running off with the cheese.

*like she had two fish hooks in the corners of her mouth with a shark hanging off each !

While Mum was gone, Dad gave me £10 to go down to a special chemist's in Clapham to buy him

It's strong stuff apparently, which is why it can only be bought from this one shop and why Dad insisted I wore gloves. It was a mission to get to Clapham.

'Are you sure I'm old enough to take two buses and walk down the high street alone?' I asked.

'Oh yes,' said Dad. I don't think he cared what danger I was in, so long as he got his hair-dye.

'What if I get attacked by an escaped and wounded bear?' I asked. 'That can be fatal.'

'Ring the zoo,' he said. 'That's what they're there for.'

I left the house just before Mel. She was wasting time waiting for you-know-who by powdering her nose in the downstairs loo, so I nicked her elf costume from her bag. Three minutes later, when Gabriel walked round the corner, Mel came charging out of the front door with a piece of cold toast in her mouth. She was shouting to someone on her mobile phone.

'No – can't talk now. Got to get off to my really important job in the City which I've had for six years since I was nineteen!' Then, without looking up, she pretended to stumble on the pavement and fell all over Gabriel, flinging her arms around his neck and flicking her hair into his face. 'Oh, I am sorry,' she said, 'but I'm late for my really important job in the City which I've had for six years since I was nineteen.' She smiled. 'Whoops! That means I've just told you my age. Sorry.'

I made my move. 'Mel!' I called out. 'Mel, you've forgotten your outfit for work!' And I ran up and gave her the green elf costume, that she wore as Santa's helper, right in front of Gabriel. He raised his eyebrows while she went scarlet with embarrassment. 'Didn't she tell you that she's very high up in the National Elf Service?' I said. 'Must fly. Bye.' Then I flapped my arms and flew off down the road, grunting like a pig.

'Ha!' I heard Mel spit. 'If I wasn't something high up in the National Elf Service I think I would want to be a murderer. And I would start with homeless orphans who I've never met before in my entire life!'

As I was waiting for the first bus to Clapham, I happened to glance into the window of the shop behind me. It was Mr Cloutman's ironmonger's shop, and there, to my surprise and delight, next to a pair of garden shears and a tube of slug pellets, was a black box with skull and crossbones on. NEW FROM CRUDACHEM! said

~ scrooge

the sign. DIE HARD – £8. How brilliant was
that – finding the stuff Dad wanted on my
doorstep! I could keep the bus money!

Gave Dad DIE HARD and swore that I had
gone to the specialist shop in Clapham like
he'd asked. Then, with two craftily earned
pounds in my pocket, I ran off to meet the
Revengers in the Toss-Bros-Snoss-Gross loo.

RALPH'S MONEY-MAKING
PLAN FOR THE ACQUISITION OF
EMBARRASSING RUDERY

Ralph's money-making plan was
rather dangerous. We had to steal
three costumes – Santa and two elves –
then go out onto the street and
collect money for charity. Only we
wouldn't tell the donors that the
charity was ME and my war-chest, with
which I was going to buy really rude presents to embarrass my big brother and
sister.

We nicked the costumes during Mr
Cloutman's tea break. He and some of his
helpers always went outside for a ciga-
rette at eleven o'clock. They left their
costumes behind because the Toss-Bros

110

Management had told them it looked bad having Santa Claus and his elves smoking out the back of the store next to the dustbins.

Ralph had brought a bucket from home with a sign on the front that he'd written himself:

CHILDREN AT CRISSMAS — PLEASE GIVE GENROUSLY TO THIS OFFISHALL COLLECTER.

We got some very strange looks from the meat packers when we stripped off round the back of the store prior to putting our costumes on. I drew the short straw and got the Santa costume, which was uncomfortably damp in the knee region and rather smelly too. It was lucky we were outdoors and it was windy. If anyone noticed the smell I could say it was the wind blowing the stink from the big cat enclosure at Whipsnade Zoo all over South London.

I put the £2 I'd earned from Dad in the bucket so it looked like we were popular, then we walked out into the supermarket car park and shook our bucket at women with children and men with dogs. Preferred the women with children, because the dogs kept sniffing my trousers. The trouble with adults is that they're naturally suspicious. Before any of them would give us money they asked for ID.

'I'm Father Christmas,' I said. 'What more ID do you need?'

'And we're elves,' said Aaron and Ralph. 'We're with him.'

After half an hour we had nothing in our bucket, because some big kid nicked the £2 and we were too polite to stop him.

'No, help yourself,' said Ralph, while the big kid karate-chopped his neck. 'Do you want my watch?'

The
Queen

Then we got birded again. Miss Bird materialized from behind a tree, like she'd just been beamed down from the USS Enterprise. She was wearing her special constable's uniform again and ran us out of the car park. We hid in an old red phone box and pretended we were making calls to the North Pole.

TELEPHONE

hello?

'Hello, Mrs Christmas,' I said to no-one. 'Can you call the AA for me, dear? The reindeer have broken down again!' That sort of thing.

But then a stupid little girl with a squashed face and a fat friend banged on the window. 'Look!' they shouted. 'It's Father Christmas! Can we speak to you?'

I thought I could make some money out

of it. After all, that's what we were there for. 'Sure,' I said, 'but it'll cost you five quid.'

'Just to speak to you?' said the girl.

'The clock's already ticking,' I said. 'You've had one pound's worth.'

'But that's not fair!' she howled, bursting into tears and setting off her fat friend.

'All right – two quid,' I said. 'Now what do you want to say to me?' The girls kept wailing. 'One?'

By the time the girl's mother turned up we'd attracted quite a crowd. The mother was furious with us for trying to make

money out of little children.

'Ah yes,' I said, 'it's sad, but that's what Christmas has become.' She wasn't impressed. Also, she wasn't leaving until we'd made it up to them. 'How?' I asked nervously.

For the rest of the day Santa and his elves sat on a bench in the high street and listened,* to all the little children of Tooting telling us what they wanted for Christmas. I have never been so bored in all my life. And I had to do all the speaking. Whatever they teach three-year-olds in school these days, it is not the art of conversation.

Learnt later that the only reason we had such a long queue of kids was because the Grotto at Toss-Bros had been closed for the afternoon on account of some idiots nicking Santa's costume!

Back at home, shinned up the drainpipe and hid the costumes under my bed. Felt useless. A whole day trying to make money for revenges and we'd *lost* £2. It was pathetic.

We discussed emergency measures, like going carol singing with a trumpet and using it like a gun to threaten people: 'If you don't pay up we'll play it through your letter box all night.' Or dressing Mr E in his nappy again and pushing him round in a pram with a sign on the hood:

THIS IS THE SON OF DOG.
PLEASE GIVE GENEROUSLY
TO AVOID PLAGUE OF
FROGS IN YOUR HOME.

There was a pause while my incredible idea sank in.

'Or . . . we could just force Will to play pool with you again,' said Ralph. 'After all, you've beaten him once – you can do it again.'

We went downstairs to find William, but found Dad instead. He was wearing a silver-foil turban with DIE HARD underneath and was rigging up an electric fence

around the new Christmas tree. He was rewiring the fairy lights to make them live! Mum was re-decorating the tree with dead flies that she'd tipped out of a lampshade and sprayed gold.

'When the light catches their eyes,' she said, 'they sparkle like diamonds. What do you think fish would look like?'

'As tree decorations, you mean?'

'Yes,' she said.

Where do they take mothers who lose the plot?

HOME FOR
MOTHERS
WHO HAVE
LOST THE PLOT

The idea behind Dad's live fairy lights was to deliver a short, sharp electric shock to Mr E if he should pee on the tree again. The idea behind replacing the silver tinsel with barbed wire was to stop me from climbing the Matterhorn again. When Dad went upstairs to rinse out his dye we had a Christmas tree that bad-boy, barbed-wire wrestlers from the WWF would have been proud of!

The Revengers wanted to know why Dad's face was camouflaged.

'What do you mean?' I said.

'Why's it greeny-brown and streaked like that night-camouflage on a soldier's face?' they said.

'Fake-tan crisis,' I said.

'You mean you put green dye into the tan bottle as well?'

'No,' I said. 'That's the natural effect.'

'So he's spontaneously changing colour?' said Aaron. 'Like Michael Jackson, only in reverse?'

'You don't think he's trying to become a pop star, do you?' said Ralph. 'I mean, he's the same colour as that perma-tanned Welsh bloke, Tom Jones.'

'Of course he's not trying to become a pop star!' I said. 'He can't sing.'

'So what?' said Ralph. 'That's not a problem these days.'

Had just hung a couple of dog biscuits on the Christmas tree to encourage Mr E to jump up and test the electric fence, when William walked in with three mates. He'd just bought himself a new cue and was planning an afternoon of pool.

'Not on my table you're not,' I said.

'I can do what I like,' he said.

'Shall we go and tell Mum and Dad how

you forced me to buy it?'

'All right,' said William. 'What do you want?'

'A bet,' I said. 'I beat you fair and square last night. I want a rematch. Winner takes all.'

'Takes all what?' he said. 'One hundred, two hundred, three hundred pounds?'

That was a bit more than I was expecting. 'How about ten?' I said.

'I thought you said you could beat me,' smirked my big brother.

Why did I feel that I was the one being suckered? 'All right, twenty,' I said. It was a deal.

And a rather stupid one at that.

a) I did not have £20.

b) I lost.

It was close, but I lost. William won on the last shot. His mates applauded and said that I had the skill to be a great player, but I'd just been unlucky.

'Tell you what,' said William. 'We could wipe that game out and forget that you owe me twenty pounds.'

'Really?' I said.

'Of course,' he said. 'Alistair, you're my

little brother, I'm hardly going to break your legs if you don't pay me, am I? So we'll play double or quits. Straight game. Winner takes all, and the prize is this. You win, I cancel all your debt. I win, I only keep the pool table. Just remember how close you were to beating me last time. You've got a real chance, mate. Honest.'

I worked it out. I could give him £20 now and not play again, or give him the pool table worth £70 if I lost again, or play and win, keep the pool table and not owe him a penny. I think it's obvious why I played.

It was obvious why I lost again as well.

'You were pants!' said Aaron. 'And William played like a world champion.'

There was a nasty little worm inside me that thought I might have been conned,

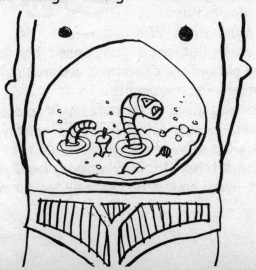

I hate goose! Not because of what it tastes like, because I've never tasted it, but because it is NOT turkey!

that William had been playing me for a patsy all along. It was a sick feeling in the pit of my stomach that got even sicker when Will and his mates picked up the pool table and took it into Will's room. 'But that's my Christmas present,' I shouted through the locked door.

'Not any more,' he said. 'And if you ever want to play on it again, Alice, you can't! It's mine! So get lost!'

Passing Mr E,  smoking gently on the carpet next to the Christmas tree, the Revengers and I ran downstairs to tell Mum what Will had done. But she'd just tinned her last mince pie before Christmas and was not in the mood for arguments.

'Nothing more to do before goosey!' she laughed ecstatically, pouring herself a large glass of wine and putting her feet up on the kitchen table. Her happiness was short-lived, however. Suddenly the air was

filled with a blood-curdling scream. It was
followed by what sounded like
wildebeest stampeding down
the stairs, and that was followed by a man with a
head like a boiled egg
bursting into the room.
It was Dad.

'Help me!' he wailed.
'My hair's fallen out!'
He turned on me like a
mad dog. 'You did go to
that specialist shop in
Clapham for the hair-
dye, didn't you?'

I had to choose my
words carefully. 'Yes,' I
lied, 'of course I did. Oh,
by the way, we're going out
carol singing. See you later.
Bye.' I couldn't think how else to
get out of there.

Mum was quick to shout out, 'I thought
you sang carols a couple of nights ago.'

'Yes, we did,' I said. 'But this is an
encore.' The Revengers looked surprised,
but followed me into the street without a
word. 'What have I done?' I said, tearing

ooh dear

DIE HARD
KILLS **ALL** WEEDS, DEAD

out my own hair. 'Whatever it was I bought Dad, it wasn't hair-dye!'

It was weedkiller. We went back and had another look in the ironmonger's window. DIE HARD – KILLS ALL KNOWN WEEDS. That's probably why it worked so successfully on Dad.

Carol singing was the only option I had left to make a quick buck, but Aaron and Ralph didn't want to come. They didn't want to miss Sun, Sand and Shagaluf on Channel 5. I told them that we were like the Three Musketeers –'All for one and one for all!' When one of us was in trouble the others always had to be there to exact revenge. They saw that they were being selfish, and after both of them had phoned home to get the programme videoed, we set off on our mission – to make money where no man had ever made money before. It is a well-known fact that strangers do not feel the pressure to give money to bad singers in quite the same way as friends and family do. So we only sang for friends and family. And a few people we hated, too. We were desperate.

Unfortunately we started with my music teacher, Mrs Muttley. She thought we were stray cats and threw uncooked cod and coley at us to stop us howling. A large fish slapped me really hard round the ear and made me yelp. She recognized my voice and opened the door.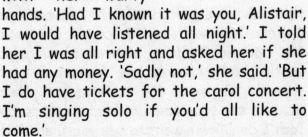

'Forgive me!' she cried, clutching her wobbly cheeks with her warty hands. 'Had I known it was you, Alistair, I would have listened all night.' I told her I was all right and asked her if she had any money. 'Sadly not,' she said. 'But I do have tickets for the carol concert. I'm singing solo if you'd all like to come.'

We accepted one ticket each, but only because that was the only way to escape from her warts.

Visiting Miss Bird held an even more unpleasant surprise. We were ripping through a lusty rendition of 'Frosty the Snowman' when Miss Bird answered the door in a leotard. It was not a pretty sight.

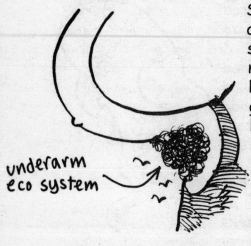

underarm eco system

She was all beak and bones and sweaty hair – and not all of it on her head. The growth under her armpits looked like she had Afroman in a headlock. Just behind her in the hall was the abdominizer that she'd confiscated off us outside Oxfam. She realized I'd seen it, slammed the door in my face, shoved an electric cattle-prod through the letterbox and shouted, 'Go away. I'm on holiday. I don't want to see you again until term starts. In fact I don't even want to see you then. And if a word of this gets out I'll have you hung, drawn, quartered and deported to Australia!'

'Can she do that?' asked Aaron.

'I think a special constable can pretty much do whatever she wants,' I said. 'That's why she nicked our presents.'

Granny Constance wouldn't even come to the front door. She just opened the top window, poured a bucket of cold water over our heads and threatened to call the Noise Police.

Ssshhh

silencer on truncheon

But when we got to Pamela Whitby's she opened the door wearing her pyjamas. She had practically no clothes on at all! It was such a lovely shock that all three of us choked on our carol and couldn't sing another note.

'If you're just going to stand there gawping at me,' she said, 'goodnight!' And she slammed the door just as I was holding out my present for her.

There was a crunch, then a cry – that was mine. I was gasping at the horror of what had just happened. Aaron rang the bell and the door was wrenched open again.

'What is it now?' she screamed.

'His present,' said Aaron.

'Sorry,' I said, peeling the flattened parcel off the door frame. 'Sorry.' Then the door was slammed for the third and final time and I returned her bent present to my pocket.

A SAD ENDING TO MY TALE OF WOE

Returned home alone, wet, cold and penniless. Therefore no embarrassing presents can be bought for dirtbag brother and sister. Therefore there will be no

Christmas payback. Therefore there can be no God, because God would not let a little child like me suffer so horribly!

Mum and Dad were drunk. Mum was 'happy drunk', having got everything ready for Christmas. Dad was 'miserable drunk', having lost all his hair. A woollen hat was his way of coping with baldness. They'd drunk so much that Mum had sprayed their supper gold and hung it on the tree. It was sausages.

'Why hasn't Mr E eaten them?' I asked.

'Ah,' said Mum. 'I'm glad you asked that, Alexstair. We have put him in the garden for all nights until the tree goes. It was him who was jumping up at the tree. We saw him do it. Jumping up for those dog biscuits someone put there.'

'Electrified lights worked brilliant!' said Dad. 'Zapped him!'

'Won't he get cold outside?' I asked.

'No,' said Mum. 'He's got a kennel. We've put him up your tent, Alanis . . . He's sleeping in that.'

'I hope he can work the zip!' said Dad.

Mum fell across the sofa in fits of giggles. 'Oh, Alistander,' she said, 'we have just watched the funniest programme ever. You'd have loved it. Sun, Sand and Shagaluf. Very funny.'

Aaaaaaaaaaaagggggggggggggghhhh!

SOME SORT OF COMPENSATION

Any programme that my parents like is NOT worth watching.

21.53 Couldn't be bothered with Operation Goose Bump tonight. Too tired. Snuggled up in bed, closed my eyes and slid my hand under my pillow. Then someone who I couldn't see hammered a nail through my little finger! Screamed and yelled until I realized I had been thwacked by a mouse-trap. Should have read the note on my headboard before I got into bed:

You are a little rat!
This is for turning Gabriel
against me.
Mel

22.02 I am a cauldron of emotions. On the one hand, I want to get revenge on my family for destroying my childhood, my innocence, my Christmas presents, my Christmas dinner, my little finger and for stealing my pool table to boot, but I haven't got the money. On the other hand, what I really love most about Christmas is kotching in front of the telly, and I haven't seen any telly all holiday. It's a question of priorities. Sometimes, when pursuing revenge relentlessly like the Terminator, one can forget the really important things in life.

TV MISSED
Cartoon Channel, 09.30: Specky Spooks
BBC2, 10.45: Wicked Witches
C4, 11.30: Gnaughty Gnomes
Really Bad Family Movies Channel, 14.00: Santa Gets the Sack!
ITV, 19.00: Charlie Chuckle's Celebrity Cracker
C5, 20.30: Sun, Sand and Shagaluf
Brrrrrm!, 23.00: Cars of the Body Snatchers

05.45 Woke early. Picked nose with little finger. When I extracted little finger, nail had gone black. Momentary panic that I had radioactive bogies. Then remembered mousetrap.

Also remembered big decision that I made last night and jumped out of bed with sense of relief. No more revenge! Suddenly life seemed so uncomplicated! Had to be downstairs before six o'clock to catch every nano-second of watchable telly. Can't wait. Prospect of full day as couch-potato very exciting.

Or should that be LEG?!

TODAY'S TV
Chocolate Box Channel, 06.00: Bumbly
Bear's Big Big Bow Tie
C4, 06.20: Tales from a Talking Tap
**BBC2, 07.00, 07.15, 07.30, 07.45, 08.00,
08.15, 08.30:** The Lampposties
C5, 08.45: Uncle Universe
BBC1, 09.00: Pete the Plasterer
BBC1, 09.30: Keith Mad's Mega Phone-In
C5, 12.30: How To . . . Kill Amphibians
Movie Mini-Max, 13.15: Rollershooter –
The Ultimate Revenge
C4, 16.00: DJ Chartman's Slice of Christmas
Boogie Cake
BBC2, 17.30: Poker School
ITV, 18.30: Stars for a Fiver!
C5, 20.00: Fatty Fart's Yuletide Loggo!
XXX Channel, 23.00: Blue Moon over
Bangkok

08.00 Vegged for two hours, then
went hunting for breakfast. Sad to see
high-security Christmas tree still intact.
Was hoping Mr E might have chanced his
arm.

Found Melanie in kitchen. She was
surprised when I didn't grass her up to
Mum about the mousetrap. But when I

133

make a decision I stick to it, and from now on it's telly, not revenge.

08.03 Noticed Mel was wearing elf costume. Asked why.

'It's complicated,' she said. 'Some costumes were stolen yesterday when Mr Cloutman was outside on his coffee break. So the manager said we all had to wear our costumes in to work today.'

'Why?' I asked.

'So that we won't have any other clothes with us,' she said. 'So we have to stay in costume all day.'

'I get it,' I said. 'So nobody can nick them.'

'I'm bored with this conversation,' said Melanie. She went into the hall to put her coat on.

* I had a go as well. It was brilliant fun. I slapped her six times before Mum pulled me off.

The doorbell rang as I was heading back towards the telly with cereal. Mel opened it. I heard her gasp. I saw her grin. I watched her faint and hit the deck like a sack of green cabbages.

Standing in the porch was Gabriel. He was holding out a letter. 'Special Delivery,' he said, as Mum rushed in from the kitchen and slapped Melanie's face.* 'I was only trying to give her this,' said Gabriel, thrusting the letter at Mum. 'Will she live?'

Mum laid Mel on the sofa, then stood up and opened the letter. Mel blinked and asked me what had happened.

'You fell over,' I said.

'That was fainting,' she said. 'He *spoke* to me.'

'He spoke to me and Mum as well, but both of us stayed upright.'

'He spoke to you?' said Mel breathlessly, sitting up and clutching my arm. 'What did he say?'

'He pointed to you lying on the floor –' I said, 'lying there in your bright-green elf costume with your pixie-acorn hat – and said, "She's a nutter, right?" And I said, "Yes."'

135

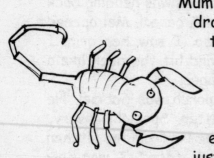

Mum screamed and dropped the letter that Gabriel had just delivered. I thought there must have been a scorpion in the envelope, but it was just a note from Dad's elder sister, Andrea, her live-in partner Graham, their seventeen-year-old daughter Mary and her ten-month-old baby, Wayne. Apparently they are coming for Christmas. Their house has blown up. Gas leak.

So why did Mum scream? Four reasons:

1) She hasn't catered for four extra people on Christmas Day.

2) The *Hello!* photographer only wants us in his photos, and NOT uninvited house-guests.

3) There's not room in the house for all of them to sleep.

4) We hate them. They are the family most unlike us in the whole world. They disapprove of everything – cars, clothes, shops, food, fun, holidays, presents, television, plastic toys and

they make their own clothes by weaving
their dogs' fur into jumpers!

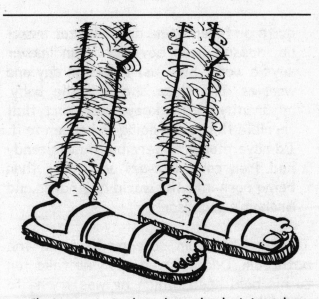

Christmas. Andrea has the hairiest legs I've ever seen on a woman.* And Graham and she aren't married, because they don't believe in ownership, they say. I say it's because he doesn't want to share his razor with her! And now their daughter Mary's got a new baby called Wayne and nobody knows who the father is, not even Mary. So Andrea and Graham are having to be Wayne's dad, which must be weird for Wayne, even though Andrea's got enough bodyhair to be a father.

Mary is just a bit older than Mel, but

quite different. She doesn't wear make-up, doesn't have boyfriends and never says a word. She just reads all day and worries. It's since she had the baby, apparently – she keeps worrying that terrible things are going to happen to it. I'd have thought a terrible thing already had. How could life get any worse than being born into the world as Andrea and Graham's grandson!

This is why Mum screamed. Up in the bathroom, Dad stopped applying fake tan to his bald head, which he was trying to stain olive-green like the rest of his face, and ran downstairs to see what was wrong. Meanwhile Mel got ready for work, William carried on sleeping and I watched more telly, because when they were coming, why they were coming and if they were coming was not really my problem.

One second later it was. The doorbell rang again. Mum swung round to face the door like she was a weedy girl-victim in a horror film and the werewolf was outside! Dad ran back upstairs. He didn't want anyone to see him.

But it wasn't a werewolf. It was worse.

It was them! Andrea was standing in the porch wearing a curtain for a dress, while Graham and Mary struggled to remove Wayne's etceteras (bath, bed, high chair, pushchair, nappies and changing mat) from the boot of the taxi. It belonged to Star Cabs. I could tell that from the rather tasteful neon star it had flashing on its roof.

'But why did you write a letter?' said Mum. 'You could have phoned and told me you were coming.'

'We don't have a phone,' said Graham. 'Andrea won't have one in the house since she read in the newspaper that the chairman of the phone company doesn't ride a bike to work.'

'Besides,' said Andrea, 'we didn't phone

because we didn't want to disturb you.'

'But you're disturbing us now!' said Mum. 'By turning up for Christmas unannounced!'

'And I thought we were family,' said Andrea with a hint of criticism in her voice.

'You are,' said Mum. 'But we've got no room to put you up!'

It wasn't as if Mum didn't try. She did, but Andrea's like a bobsleigh. Once she's set her mind on something she won't be deflected off course. 'We've only got one spare room,' Mum said.

'Nonsense,' said Andrea, sweeping into the hall on her bushy yak's legs. 'We hardly take up any space at all. You won't even know we're here. Mary and Wayne can go in with Melanie. William can move in with Alistair, Graham can have William's room and I'll take the spare room.'

'That's not fair,' I said, as Mary thrust a crate of baby food into my hands. 'Why can't you and Graham share?'

'Oh, dear me, no, Alick,' laughed Graham. 'Walked into a minefield there. Sleeping in the same room's a bit of a dark and dangerous subject these days.'

'We don't share a room any more,' said Andrea. 'Not since the arrival of the

140

Graham Whale.'

'The Graham Whale?' I asked.

'Have you never heard a whale snore, Alistair?'

I have sinus trouble, that's why...

'Ah. So Graham snores.'

'Like a tractor,' she said. 'Plus, we don't share a room because, without being indelicate, we don't want another unwanted child in this family, do we?'

Even I knew that that was a horrible thing to say. Everyone else must have felt the same, because we all looked at Mary and smiled sympathetically, as if to say, 'We don't mind your unwanted baby.' But Mary didn't seem bothered at all.

'I mean,' said Andrea, 'look how hard you have to fight to be loved, Alistair. It wouldn't be fair to inflict that on another child, would it?' She meant me! I was the unwanted child! And why was Mum blushing?

Mel fell in love with the baby, Wayne. She picked him up and cuddled him like he was hers. 'He's gorgeous,' she said. 'You're so clever, Mary.'

'She had him at home in the airing cupboard,' said Andrea, poking Mary in the ribs. 'She never says a word so I have to speak for her. It was the only place we could find that matched her womb.'

There's information you need to know and information you don't. Personally, I did not need to know that Mary's womb was full of towels, sheets and a hot water boiler. But Mel was lapping it up and talking in a stupid dreamy voice. 'Ooh, I wish

---

I had a younger brother,' she said.
  'Hello!' I shouted. 'You do!'
  'No, not you,' she said. 'A nice one!'

BIG NOTE NUMBER 1

Whatever feelings I might have had about stopping revenge in order to watch tons of telly are now entirely reversed!

I hated the baby. Especially since everyone wanted me to hold it all the time – we looked so sweet together, they said. The second I lifted it up and draped it over my shoulder, what does it do?* Pukes down my back! A great white splatter like an albatross's poop. It smelled like pongy cheese as well. Disgusting!

  'I think it will do Alistair a power of good to look after a baby,' said Andrea. 'Boys these days have their heads filled with macho nonsense morning, noon and night. Real men –' she looked at Graham with his hand-knitted tank top and patchy moustache – 'real men are in touch with their feminine sides.'

BIG NOTE NUMBER 2

Must check myself in bath for signs of boobs.

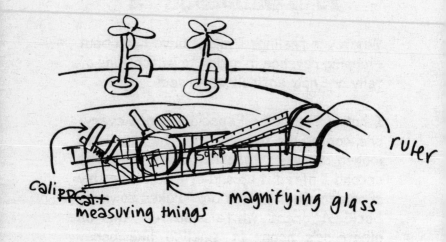

calipers
measuring things
magnifying glass
ruler

Dad came down eventually wearing a cream-coloured Beanie Hat. Andrea and Graham stood there and laughed.

'Your face has changed colour,' said Graham. 'Oh, I get it. You're playing a king in the school Nativity.'

'No,' said Dad.

'So why the turban?'

Andrea and Graham call the telly 'Satan's Eyeball'.

'I like wearing trendy streetwise hats,' said Dad.

'You look ridiculous!' said Andrea. 'Like ram dressed as lamb.'

Mum wasn't listening to any of this. She was still worrying about Christmas Day. 'No, you can't stay,' she said. 'I've only got one goose. There won't be enough food, and it'll look like I serve mean portions in Hello!'

Andrea's ears pricked up. 'Hello!?' she said. 'That awful magazine?' She tutted loudly. 'Anyway, Celia, as you very well know, we're vegetarians.'

'So you don't have to worry about us,' said Graham. 'We're no trouble. Dips, crisps, potatoes, veg, soup, bread, pud, custard, cream, cheese, wine, beer, salmon, trifle, sandwiches, bubbly and oysters is all we ask for on Christmas Day. I must be the luckiest man alive. My Christmas dinner is being cooked by Celia Fury!'

So while Mum went back to the shops, Mel went off to work, and Dad woke William and washed sheets, I was forced to entertain our guests in the sitting room. So TV off and cards out.

'Do you know Beggar My Neighbour, Alick?'

'Alistair,' I said. And, yes, I did know Beggar My Neighbour, the most boring game since International Ironing.

So rather cleverly I said, 'No, I don't know it, Uncle Graham. I know Draw the Well Dry, but you don't want to play that, do you? Sorry.'

Graham roared with laughter and rubbed his hands together gleefully. 'But they're the same game, you chump! Can you believe that?' No, actually, I couldn't. 'Lady Luck must love you, you young cowboy! So come on, Alick, deal away!'

Mum got home three hours later. By then I was desperate to escape from Graham and his cards. I'd just lost the sixteenth game in a row when he beat my three kings with a single jack.

'Not often seen that move,' said Graham. 'Jack high! Watch and learn, Alick. Another?'

'I couldn't,' I said, as I heard a key rattle in the front door. 'I've got to help Mum with the shopping.' For the first time ever I rushed out to carry her bags. I left Graham getting stuck into Clock Patience and Mary and Andrea getting stuck into Wayne's fifth nappy in an hour. Never thought I'd

say this, but I've just met something that smells worse than Mr E.

Was helping Mum unpack in the kitchen when Andrea and Graham walked in and hovered. Mum started slamming boxes of eggs onto the table. I felt uneasy.

'May we have a word?' said Andrea finally. Mum stopped, but didn't look pleased. 'It's about Christmas Day,' Andrea said, 'and Hello! magazine. We think it's wrong that you've invited them here. Christmas is about family, Celia, not making money from a set of tacky photographs in a magazine full of celebrity gossip and tittle-tattle.'

I'd never noticed before, but when Mum gets angry her nostrils swell like two tiny beach balls. I hate arguments between grown-ups, so tried to make myself invisible behind a slatted chair.

'Christmas is also about making a living, Andrea,' hissed Mum. 'Not something you've ever had to worry about. And if I don't sell my books, we don't eat, we don't go on holiday—'

'What do you need a holiday for?' said Andrea. 'Do what we do. Take two weeks off and clean out the loft. Much better for you. Put up some wind chimes. You'll think you're in Bali.'

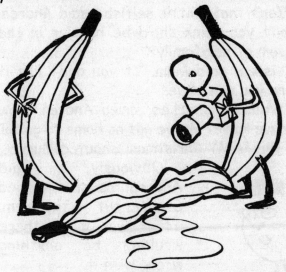

Mum took a deep breath and squeezed the life out of a banana. *'Hello!* ARE coming on Christmas Day, whether you like it or not,' she said.

'Well, that's the whole thing,' said Graham. 'We don't like it, Celia. That's what Andrea's been trying to tell you. You haven't been listening.'

'Oh, and another thing,' said Andrea. 'I gather my mother – your husband's mother too, in case you've forgotten – will be spending Christmas alone.'

'Yes,' said Mum. 'On a luxury cruise ship up the Nile.'

'Isn't that a little selfish?' said Andrea. 'Don't you think she'd be happier in the bosom of her family?'

'Listen,' said Mum. 'If you don't like it here you can leave.'

'Well, I'm shocked,' cried Andrea. 'How can we leave? We've got no home to go to!'

'This is MY Christmas!' shouted Mum.

'Obviously,' said Andrea, as she hurried Graham out of the room. 'If it was mine, there wouldn't be anything wrong with it.'

Fortunately that was when the doorbell rang for the end of Round One. It was a lady called Mrs Shepherd from Social Services. She came bearing gifts of powdered milk for baby Wayne.

Spent afternoon unable to watch TV while Mary taught Wayne the capital

cities of the world and Andrea practised her violin. Made regular trips to hall to check my ears weren't bleeding. William stayed upstairs all day playing pool and Mum refused to come out of the kitchen.

17.15 When Mel got home we made the beds and sorted out who was sleeping where. It was like Andrea said: Wayne and Mary went in with Mel, Graham had William's room, and I got William. On account of William's stinky Super Poopers I am seriously considering relocating into the tent outside. If anyone's going to lose a night's sleep it's Mr E. He can sleep on the patio.

17.45 Mum far too frazzled to make supper at home. We are going out. Everyone happy except Andrea*. Who would babysit Wayne? My hand went up first. Everyone made the usual objections about me being too young and irresponsible, but Andrea thought it was high time I learnt how to be an adult, and overruled them. Yes! I could watch the telly in peace.

Mary insisted I went upstairs with her to put Wayne to bed, so she could show me how to work the two-way baby alarm. It

* surprise surprise!

151

was just like a walkie-talkie.

'It's good if you talk to him from downstairs,' she said, 'because you're male and not having a father he's not used to male voices. So feel free to say what you want. Only no swearing!' Then she showed me how to change a nappy. I pretended to watch, but I wasn't plunging my hands into that under ANY circumstances. No way! Then I had to sit there for half an hour while Mary read 'The Nativity Story' to Wayne and he went off to sleep.

At the end of the story Mary leaned over the cot and kissed Wayne goodnight. 'Who's my best boy?' she said. 'Wayne is. Yes he is. You are good enough to eat. Yes you are. As scrummy as a lubbly lump of Cheddar cheese.'

I think she thinks he's a dog.

'That makes him little baby cheeses,' I joked, but Mary didn't get it. For me, however, it was like suddenly I'd seen that blinding light that everyone godly talks about. I looked at Wayne again and gulped. He looked like any other baby – fat, dribbling, scabby-headed – but I knew he was different. It was obvious. The signs were all there. He had no father, his mother was called Mary, Gabriel brought the news of his imminent arrival, he travelled under a star, there was no room when they got here, I turned

up three kings at cards, and a shepherd has just come bearing gifts!

i.e. she threatened to come round and bore me all night about the time I climbed the Christmas tree

'He's asleep now,' said Mary. 'Shall we go?'

I swear as I left the room I saw a little halo.

After they'd all gone the phone rang. It was Granny Constance. 'Where is everyone?' she snapped. 'And what's that?' Wayne was making baby noises on the walkie-talkie.

'Er, nothing,' I said. I didn't know if I was allowed to tell her that Andrea was here or not. 'I've got the telly on.'

'You're lying,' she said. 'I can always tell.' Then, by some sort of telephone hypnosis, she forced me to reveal that it was Wayne crying, and that Andrea's family was staying for Christmas. 'But I thought you were having a quiet Christmas,' she said.

'We were,' I said. 'It was just us and *Hello!* and now we've got Andrea too.'

'*Hello!*'

'You didn't know about *Hello!*?' I said.

She did not. And now I'd gone and told her. Not only that, but she told me to tell Mum that she was cancelling the Nile and rejoining her family for Christmas. What had I done? Mr Popular Trousers had struck again. Mum was going to hate me!

154

I put the unknowable future out of my mind and concentrated on the glorious present. Phoned Revengers. 'For he's a jolly good fellow, for he's a jolly good fellow, for he's a jolly good fe-e-llow, who Judas will deny.'

'Ralph!' shouted the Reverend Ming. 'It's that idiot friend of yours again!'

I thought vicars were supposed to be friendly.

'What do you want?' said Ralph. 'Do you know what's on telly?'

'What I've got to tell you is bigger than any telly programme,' I said.

'It's *Star for a Fiver!*' he said. He was right. *Star for a Fiver!* is a brilliant programme. Washed-up celebrities pay £5 to get their faces on the telly again by singing a song in a foreign language.

'Forget it,' I said. 'This is bigger than the world, Ralph. It's historical. You've got to come over.'

'I can't,' he said. 'It's Dad's carol concert. He says I've got to go.'

'No, that's perfect,' I said. 'I'll phone Aaron and we'll meet you there.'

Half an hour later I arrived at the church with Wayne wrapped up in three blankets and a balaclava.

'What's that?' said Aaron.

'Well, it looks like a baby,' I said, 'but it isn't.'

'Hurry up!' said Ralph. 'Mrs Muttley's over halfway through her medley and Dad'll notice I've gone.'

I could hear Mrs Muttley's shrill voice piercing the five-metre-thick stone walls. Clouds of bats flew in swirling clusters around the gravestones as if driven mad by her high-pitched caterwauling.

'This baby,' I said, as the moon came out from behind a cloud and flooded the church in heavenly light, 'is the New Messiah!' Mrs Muttley hit a top C and smashed the stained-glass window behind the altar.

'What's that?' said Aaron.

'Like Jesus' little brother,' I said. That did it. Now they were impressed! I told them how I knew and asked them how we could use this discovery to our best advantage.

'Well, there must be money in it,' said Aaron. 'After all, Jesus' little brother is not something you see every day of the week. And if we could sell Wayne's story to the papers for a hundred pounds you could buy your really rude presents and our Christmas revenge would be complete!'

We used Ralph's mobile to phone the Tooting Tribune. We spoke to a real journalist who obviously knew his business.

'Are you sure it's the New Messiah?' he said. 'I mean, does he have a halo?'

'Funny you should mention that,' I said. 'Yes.'

'Don't tell me,' he said. 'Is it a blue haze that hovers over his bum just before a nappy change?' Then he broke into peals of laughter. It turned out that the paper was only interested in the story if either the Archbishop of Canterbury said that Wayne was the younger Son of God, or the baby could perform a miracle. I told them I'd see what I could do and phone tomorrow.

After the service was over, Ralph took me to meet his father, who was the only person we could think of who might know the Archbishop of Canterbury. When I told him my name he looked at me like I was something squidgy he'd just stepped in on the pavement. I asked him politely if he thought he could get the Archbishop of Canterbury down tonight to verify that Wayne was the younger Son of God, but he said no. He didn't believe my proof. So I tried a different tack.

'Reverend Ming,' I said, 'I'm going to be honest here, if I may. The main reason we're doing this is for money.' Ralph rolled his eyes in his head and groaned. 'So if I was to hire the baby to you for an hour or so, on temporary loan obviously, because his mum doesn't know I'm here, how much would you give me? Bear in mind that you could use him in Christmas ads for the church, crib scenes, opening super-markets, that sort of thing.'

'No,' said Ralph's father.

'It's for a good cause,' I said. 'To buy rude presents to pay back my big brother and sister for wrecking my childhood.'

'Get out,' he said, 'and never darken my doors again.'

'All right,' I said, 'I'm sorry. How about

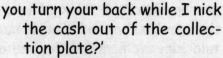

you turn your back while I nick the cash out of the collection plate?'

The Reverend Ming obviously did not have his forgiving Christian socks on, because he chucked us out. Not Ralph, obviously – as his son he had to stay – but we made signs to him that we'd meet him in the morning to perform some miracles.

Met Pamela Whitby as the congregation came out.

'Happy Christmas,' I said, shoving Wayne's pushchair across her path so she had to stop. 'Pamela, I've been trying to give you this all week.' I slid the battered package out of my pocket. 'It's a present.'

'You want a kiss, don't you?' she said.

'No!' I protested.

'Because I don't kiss rude boys,' she said. 'Especially not ones who try to buy my affections.' And she strode off, leaving me standing there like a prune.

Mrs Muttley saw me. 'Oh Alistair, you came!' she trilled. 'And

you've brought me a present!' She
snatched the package out of my hand and
opened it. 'Oh! Bits of broken bracelet . . .
How lovely!' Then she took my cheeks
between her warty hands and gave me
another disgusting wet kiss. If she thinks,
just because she's taken a gift off me,
that we are now boyfriend and girlfriend,
I am NEVER having another piano lesson in
my life!

Aaron, Wayne and I walked each other
home. Tomorrow it was miracle or bust.
Either I got the money off that newspaper
or my revenge was dead.

'We could always write a
book about baby Wayne,'
said Aaron. 'Call it The
Bibful and sell millions of
copies all over the
world.' But there wasn't
really time for all that.

I got home and put
Wayne to bed just
before the others got
back.

'Was he any trouble?' asked Mary.

'No,' I said. 'Slept like a baby.' Then I
remembered Granny's phone call and asked

Mum if I could have a word in private. She was furious when I told her that Granny was coming on Christmas Day too.

'How am I going to feed them all?' she cried. 'What am I going to do with them while Hello! are taking photographs?'

'Lock them in the garden shed?' I suggested.

But Mum really was upset and called me a stupid, selfish boy, which seemed a bit harsh. Anyway, that brought Beanie Man in to see what all the noise was about, and William and Mel came in after him to see why he was shouting. Once the whole family was involved I didn't stand a chance. I was sent to Coventry for being a prawnhead.

Didn't go as far as Coventry, though. Just popped outside into the tent with Mr E. At least he couldn't tell me off, and it was quite comforting having my ears licked.

As I was going to sleep, William and Mel put their heads out of their windows and shouted, 'Goodnight, Christmas wrecker!'

'That's rich coming from you,' I shouted back. 'Childhood wreckers!'

'Will you three shut up!' shouted Mum. 'You're all as bad as each other!'

'Will everyone shut up!' screamed Dad.

I know the smell well, because Mr E rolls in dead furry things at least once a week.

'Some of us are trying to get some sleep before our tanning bed tomorrow!'

Nice family. Nice Christmas spirit.

I was so traumatized that I had a horrible dream about Father Christmas crashing his sleigh on an iceberg. He was marooned in the freezing cold with his stinking reindeer and had to curl up next to them to keep warm. Their stink was so bad that it even woke me up. In fact it turned out it was Mr E who was smelling. The dirty little pug was curled up against my stomach, having just rolled in the carcass of a dead badger!

Stink or no stink, I was too proud to go back inside the house. At least, I thought

I was. Mel suddenly pushed her way into the tent. She was joining me, apparently, because the horrible baby was crying.

'Phwaw! Your farts smell disgusting!' she gasped.

'That's dead badger,' I said.

'Well, you shouldn't eat it, should you?' she said. 'By the way, Alice, do you think I look tragic today?'

'You always look tragic,' I said. 'Why today?'

'Because today I am a victim,' she said. 'Because of the robbery at work, I've spent the whole day being interviewed by the police who've treated me like a common criminal. Poor me!'

'You're just sounding pathetic because you want my sleeping bag,' I said.

'No I'm not,' she said. 'I was just going to take it anyway.' Then she dragged me out of the bag and jumped in herself. I didn't mind sharing my tent with the freezing cold, Mr E, or even the bad badger smell, but my big sister – not a chance!

Met Mary in the kitchen giving wailing Wayne a drink of water.

'Try this,' I said, handing her a cork. 'Bung it in his gob and he'll never cry again!'

They say that elephants have got long memories. If that is so I must be a woolly mammoth!

Mary did not find me amusing.

Then, after she and Wayne had gone back to bed, this 'stupid, selfish boy' taught Mum her long-overdue lesson. I completed Operation Goose Bump by chucking the goose over the garden wall. Finally I braved my own bedroom, where William had turned the air a darker shade of purple.

01.15 Thought for the day: have paid back Mum and Dad. Now it's big brother and sister's turn!

TV MISSED
BBC2, 08.00, 08.15, 08.30: The Lampposties
C5, 08.45: Uncle Universe
BBC1, 09.00: Pete the Plasterer
BBC1, 09.30: Keith Mad's Mega Phone-In
C5, 12.30: How To . . . Kill Amphibians
Movie Mini-Max, 13.15: Rollershooter –
The Ultimate Revenge
C4, 16.00: DJ Chartman's Slice of Christmas
Boogie Cake
BBC2, 17.30: Poker School
ITV, 18.30: Stars for a Fiver!
C5, 20.00: Fatty Fart's Yuletide Loggo!
XXX Channel, 23.00: Blue Moon over
Bangkok

TODAY'S TV
Cartoon Channel, 09.00: Evil Dr Star and
the Christmas Tree
ITV, 11.00: Presenters Do the Strangest
Things in Front of Cameras at Christmas
Shopping Channel, 11.30: Last Minute
Christmas Shopping
BBC2, 17.30: Christmas Carols from
Christmas Island
ITV, 18.30: Cilla's Christmas Surprise
BBC1, 19.30: A Christmas Hamper of
Humiliating Christmas Home Movies!
Comedy Channel, 20.00: Fanny McFunny's
Funny Old Christmas Show
BBC1, 21.00: Auntie's Old Christmas
Chestnuts
C5, 22.00: Christmas Cheerleaders

Busy morning at Last Chance Saloon. Mum
freaked at the disappearing goose. After
long discussion we decided there were only
two explanations. Either it had grown feathers and flown away, or it had been taken by
the sneaky fox. At the mention of the word
'fox', Mary had a fit of the nervy-hubjubs.
She said she knew she was being silly, but
she couldn't stop imagining a red foxy muz-
zle slipping through the bars of Wayne's cot,

picking him up by his nappy and whisking him off to its den for a midnight feast.

I told her she was being silly, because there wasn't a beast on the planet that would carry Wayne off by his nappy. The stink would put them off. 'Except for rats,' I said, 'because they live on poo, don't they? So to them Wayne's nappy would probably be like a delicious picnic.'

Mary reacted to the idea of rats devouring her precious baby by leaving the house in tears and going in search of festive joy. Mel took her to Toss-Bros so Wayne could meet Father Christmas for the first time.

Then, while Andrea ate toast like a horse and dropped so many crumbs on her hairy legs that I thought she must be feeding them, Dad went off to have his Christmas sunbed.

'What I'm doing,' he told me, 'is activating this fake tanning lotion to give me an all-over bronzing like Adonis.' As for his bald head, he was going to shine it up and turn it into a feature. 'Look at Bruce Willis,' he said. 'Women like bald men.'

'No they don't,' I told him. 'They like Bruce Willis.'

Mum put her coat on again and dragged herself off to the supermarket to cater for Granny and no goose. I did say I'd go with her, but she insisted on being alone. Actually, I knew she was going to say that, otherwise I wouldn't have offered!

Before she went she gave me £30 to take dead-badger-loving Mr E to the poodle parlour for a wash and scrub up.

She didn't know it, but she had just handed me the answer to my gift crisis. Who needed miracles? All I had to do was clean up Mr E on my own and keep the money. She'd never know!

So while Will slept in and Andrea and Graham removed the barbed wire and electrocuting lights from the Christmas tree, I phoned the Revengers and asked them to help me wash a dog.

Rewind to Andrea and Graham. They are tree-huggers. They believe that every living thing in the universe has a soul and that includes dead Christmas trees. So they waited till Mum and Dad were out of the house before liberating our tree and setting its needles free! Personally I think there are more important things to worry about in this world – like are we going to get turkey for Xmas lunch or not?

Revengers and me used Dad's hair-clippers* to trim the lumpy bits out of Mr E's fur. Unfortunately he wouldn't stand still, so we kept taking off more than we meant to until he looked like a scabby old teddy bear. We couldn't shave every-where, because we were scared of

169

chopping off his ears and tail, so in between the bald patches, on the top of his head and round his down-belows, he had random bushes of fur, like he was covered in moustaches. We had not improved his look.

We gave him a bath, soaped him all over, rinsed him down and dried him with Mum's hairbrush and hairdryer. We were trying to cover his bald patches by staightening the remains of his fur to make it longer, but he was starting to look like a Pekinese and I hate them even more than I hate pugs. So we stopped while Aaron had thebright idea that maybe curling the fur would make his coat look thicker. We used Mum's curling tongs, but only managed to singe little clumps, which in the end we had to cut off.

After half an hour we gave up. Mr E smelled a lot nicer, but he looked like a small, woollen loo-roll cover that had been mostly eaten by moths.

'What do we do?' panicked Ralph.

'Blame the poodle parlour,' I said.

Luckily, when Mum got home she was so upset by the undecorated Christmas tree that she didn't notice Mr E. Andrea and Graham lectured Mum on how hurtful it was to the tree's feelings to dress it up in barbed wire.

'Besides,' said Graham, 'I'm sure Alick is old enough now not to climb the tree and smash your ornaments.'

'The barbed wire wasn't meant for Alistair!' screamed Mum. 'It was for Mr E.'

'Oh,' said Graham. 'Well, that's worse. Poor dumb creature like that, he could have got hurt.'

'Alistair wouldn't have got hurt,' Mum said.

'I was talking about Mr E,' said Graham.

Mum swung the turkey at Graham to get him out of her way. Apparently they'd run out of geese in the shops.

DID YOU
SAY TURKEY,
ALISTAIR?
YES!
'Swung the
TURKEY!'

Yum Yum! !

Operation Goose Bump has been a spectacular success and I have been a spectacular mastermind. I am an evil genius!

Wonder if they do greetings cards for evil geniuses? If so, must send myself a congratulations card.

At this point I thought I was home and dry with the £30. Me and the Revengers were just about to leave the house to shop for rude presents for Will and Mel, when we heard a scream from the bathroom. It was Mum. She'd just found all the fur that we'd cut off Mr E. We thought we'd done a good job of hiding it in the bin under several layers of tissues, but obviously not. She screamed because she thought it was a rat, but when she kicked the bin and it didn't move she realized it was fur. Then she realized whose.

'Is this Mr E's fur?' she yelled at me, while the Revengers cringed outside the door.

They said it was like waiting to see the head-teacher

'No,' I lied. 'It's not Mr E's. I took him to the poodle parlour, just like you said. I think it might be someone else's.'

'Whose?' she said.

'I saw Aunty Andrea coming in here,' I said. 'Maybe she shaved her legs.' But Mum wasn't buying it. And I wasn't buying rude presents either. Had to return the £30.

When I came out of the bathroom the Revengers knew what had happened.

'Only a miracle will save us now,' I said. So we phoned the Tooting Tribune and told

173

them to meet us near the boating pond on the common.

'Why?' said Aaron.

'Sea of Galilee,' I said. Then we nipped downstairs and threw two sets of waterwings, a length of hose, the last three bottles of white wine from Dad's cellar, an extra-large nappy, a feeding bottle full of water, one wineglass, a corkscrew and some seal-tight plastic bags into a rucksack.

'All we need now is Wayne,' said Ralph.

'Bum!' I said. 'I forgot about him.'

And Wayne wasn't at home.

Luckily for us Mel got the sack. Toss-Bros let her go because Santa's Grotto had to close a day early on account of there being no Father Christmas. Without the red costume to wear, Mr Cloutman was sent home. This meant that five minutes after we realized we didn't have the miracle baby, Mel came home in tears. It also meant that Mary came home in tears, because Wayne hadn't met Santa and it was all her fault. I moved in like a weasel.

'You look upset,' I said to Mary. 'Would it help you if I took Wayne off your hands for an hour? Took him for a walk in the park?' Everyone looked at me as if I was a saint. 'Well, it is Christmas,' I said. 'The season of goodwill to all men.'

When we got outside into the street we legged it to the boating pond, so that we

Scrooge

could set up our miracle before the man from the Tooting Tribune turned up. Wayne's pushchair did 0–60 in about 8.3 seconds!

What we did to Wayne was this. We filled the plastic bag with white wine, then inserted the hosepipe into the wine and sealed the top of the bag around the pipe so that nothing spilled out. Then we put him in the extra-large nappy, slid the wine bag inside, poked the hosepipe out of a leg hole, and zipped him back into his snow-suit.

When the reporter arrived Wayne was asleep. 'So is this the Younger Son of God?' he said.

'It is,' I said. 'He's called Wayne. Have you got the hundred pounds?'

'Oh no,' he said, 'not until I've seen this miracle.'

'All right,' I said. 'Water into wine. Wayne, you have three minutes. Do your stuff!' Wayne was still asleep so I gently shook him awake and pressed the bottle of water to his lips. He took three sips, then fell asleep again. 'Behold!' I said. 'Regard the miracle.' I unzipped his snow-suit and put the wine glass by the leg hole of his nappy, then pressed down on the wine bag inside. It squirted out like a fountain. And when I gave it to the reporter his face fell a mile.

'It is wine,' he said. 'Pucker stuff 'n' all! I'll have some more, if you don't mind.'

'Wayne's pleasure,' I said. 'And then the hundred pounds.'

But this time I must have pressed too hard, because the pipe came out of the bag and shot out the leg of the nappy, and when I tried to catch it I stumbled into the bench and knocked off the rucksack, and the two bottles of unopened wine rolled out and smashed.

The second he saw them the reporter was off. 'You're wasting my time!' he shouted.

'You got a glass of wine out of it,' said Ralph.

'You can't go yet,' I called. 'We haven't done walking on water yet.'

'And it took me ages to blow up the water wings!' shouted Aaron.

On the way home Wayne filled his nappy.

'Do you really think he's the Younger Son of God?' asked Aaron.

'Not any more,' I said. 'Phwaw!' It was a miracle any of us survived the pong.

The taste of failure was a bit like Granny's marmalade – bitter and hard to swallow! The Revengers had never failed on a mission before. But the stark facts were these: we hadn't got the money and there were only a few hours left till the shops closed.

'Right,' I said. 'There's nothing else for it. I've been saving my secret idea for just this occasion. Revengers, it's the pudding!' They looked at me like they didn't know what I was talking about. That was because they didn't.

There was chaos at home when we got back. Dad had fallen asleep on his sunbed and was suffering from third-degree burns, which meant he was going to have to go into hospital overnight.

'Is it serious?' I asked.

'No,' said Mum. 'You know what your dad's like. Bumps his toe and think he's broken his leg.'

'Is he going to be in hospital tomorrow?'

'Probably,' she said. 'But that's not a surprise. Nothing else has gone right this Christmas, has it?'

Dad's skin had gone weird. Patches of it were red where he was sunburnt, but his face had gone all wrinkled where he'd rubbed in that fake tan. He looked like an old man, an old Indian man with a bald head.

'Still,' I said, 'at least if he's in hospital he won't be in the pictures.'

'That is a blessing,' said Mum.

'If my mates saw him looking like that,' I said, 'I'd die of embarrassment. They'd think my dad was Mahatma Gandhi.'

Mum and Will took Dad into hospital, so Mum could get Will's verruca seen to while she was there. It'd changed again. It didn't look like Moby Dick any more. Now it bore a striking resemblance to the Prime Minister's wife. When Dad left,

OOOH! do you think so?

I ♥ TONY

lying flat out in the boot of the car, he was crying for himself. All he'd ever wanted was his picture in *Hello!*, and now he'd blown it big time.

'Bye-bye, everyone. I love you. Happy Christmas.' Those were his parting words. 'Namaste, Dad.' Those were mine.

With Mum and Dad gone I whipped the Revengers into the kitchen, where I revealed my last-ditch plan – to nick the money out of the Christmas pudding. We had to get on with it before someone came in, so we took the direct route to the money. We tipped the pudding out of the bowl and crumbled it into hundreds of little bits so that all the silver coins fell out.

'Won't your mum be suspicious,' asked Aaron, 'if there's no money inside when she serves it?' He had a point.

'Last year,' I said, 'William got the blame, because he left his rugby socks inside. So all we've got to do is plant some incriminating evidence.' And I knew exactly what that was.

'She won't miss them,' I told the Revengers as we stuffed Mel's red tights into the pudding bowl. 'They're not the tights she normally wears. She's just bought them for tomorrow.' Then I replaced the silver foil lid on the bowl so no-one would know we'd been there, and scooped the coins into my hands. Unfortunately, we couldn't count the money there and then, because Andrea and Graham came into the kitchen to make some radish and fennel sandwiches for supper*. So we went outside into the tent and counted it there.

To say we were gutted would not be accurate. After all that work, the silver coins were silver six-pences – they went out of use with penny farthings! Worth ZILCH! How typical was that of my mum? Her mum used sixpences so she had to use sixpences. Why couldn't she have modernized and used £5 notes?

CHRISTMAS
R.I.P.
THE END

That was it. I had to accept that I was now living in a revenge-free zone, that all the injustices perpetrated on me by William and Mel would go unpunished. It stuck in my gullet! I'd paid Mum and Dad back, but the real demons at the feast, the real evil ones who had told me that Father Christmas didn't exist, had opened my presents, stolen my pool table and squashed my finger in a mousetrap were going to get away scot-free.

'Not scot-free,' said Ralph. 'Will and Mel still think the wrapped-up boxes round the tree contain their presents. But they don't, do they? So when you're generously handing out your presents, Alistair, they won't be handing out anything! And Hello! will be recording their Scrooge-like mean-ness on camera!'

Why do I always end up doing fussy girl's stuff?

'One problem,' I said. 'I haven't got any presents. I broke them all.'

'Well, you've got to have presents,' said Ralph, 'otherwise it won't work. You'll just have to make something.'

'Granny Constance once taught me how to make fudge,' I said without enthusiasm.

'So make fudge,' he said, with a devil in his eye. 'And while you're at it pop a little curry powder in!'

'Curry fudge?' I said.

oh dear, I think I'm going to be busy

'Slip a chunk to Mel and Will and all your Christmas problems will be over,' he smiled.

'And Andrea and Graham,' I said, 'because they've stopped me watching telly. And Granny Constance for throwing a bucket of water over us when we were carol singing.'

'Now you're cooking,' said Ralph. Not yet, but I would be!

Aaron had been quiet for several minutes. Suddenly, he leapt up as if he'd just sat on an electric eel. 'Have you still

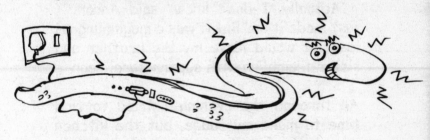

got that Santa costume?' he asked. It was under my bed. 'Why don't you put it on tonight, then creep into Mel and Will's bedrooms?'

'Why?' I asked.

'Your dad's in hospital and he's the one who usually does the stockings, right? So, if Father Christmas appears to your brother and sister while your dad's asleep ten miles away, they're going to think that

Father Christmas really does exist! And that is going to mess with their minds worse than psychedelic rap!'

'What's psychedelic rap?' asked Ralph.

'Actually, I don't know,' said Aaron. 'I just made it up.' But it was a megamungous idea! It would leave my big brother and sister trembling with supernatural fear!

All through the evening I tried to find time to make my fudge, but the kitchen was always full of people and for obvious reasons I didn't want anyone to see what I was doing. If it wasn't Mum de-gutting the turkey, it was Andrea and Graham making more nettle sandwiches or the write-a-letter-to-Santa marathon.

It is a tradition on Christmas Eve that William, Mel and I sit together at the kitchen table with a loo-roll and write our wish lists to Santa. This year Wayne joined us and Mary wrote his first letter.

Dear Father Christmas,

My name is Wayne and I am nearly one year old. If you don't mind, I would prefer not to have presents this year, because presents break and are not sound investments for my future. What I'd really like is a Savings Bond for £100 so that I can start a fund for my University Education.

Yours truly,
Wayne

This letter was poetry in comparison to my big brother and sister's.

Dear Father Christmas,
Been drunk all year and hate being so childish. If you don't bring me anything ever again I shan't miss a wink of sleep.
Melanie Fury

Dear FC,
Racing Car.
Fit Chick.
'A's in all my exams.
Ta
Wills

Mine, on the other hand, contained a hint of the betrayal that I felt towards everyone on the Father Christmas front. I cannot deny that it was flecked with bile and rancour and a little bit of bitterness as well.

Dear Father Christmas - or should I call you Dad?

How are you? Skin not too burnt? Hair growing nicely? Like hospital food, do you? Don't expect you'll be able to bring me anything from your sick bed, will you? What I would really like this year is a mini-tornado to sweep through my big brother and sister's bedrooms and whip them off to the end of the rainbow like Dorothy in The Wizard of Oz (BBC1, 11.25, Christmas Day). Only don't make it be a dream like it is in the film. MAKE IT REAL! What I DON'T want is a bottle of fake tan, because I've seen what a mess it's made of your face. You'll be glad to hear that we've got turkey tomorrow after all. Like me you prefer it to goose, don't you? Well, tough, because you won't be eating it!

Love to the reindeer and the elves.

Love,
Alistair

PS Does Rudolf have a red nose because he spent too long on the sunbed as well?

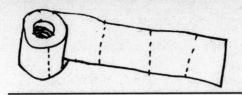

Mine was so long that I finished all the paper on the loo-roll. Then we lit a fire in the sitting room, waited for the chimney to get hot and released our letters with tongs. Unfortunately there was so much paper that the letters were too heavy to fly and got stuck halfway up. We had to poke them up the rest of the way with a broomstick. I made a joke that Granny would get a hot bottom when next she sat on it. But nobody got it. Or if they did, nobody laughed.

Suddenly there was a cry for help from the loo upstairs. Graham had sat down without checking for paper and we'd just sent it all up the chimney! Mum thought this was hysterical, but Andrea didn't.

'I didn't realize you and Graham used paper,' Mum said. 'In fact I didn't know you used toilets, Andrea. I thought you just dug a pit in the garden and used leaves!'

Andrea left the room in a huff. It's going to be such a lovely day tomorrow!

Usual stocking fight over Dad's socks. William and Mel ended up with the nice clean ones. I got the smelly one that Dad has kept from the last game of football he ever played at school. He says preserving it exactly as it was* keeps him young. It keeps me awake.

I DON'T NEED a pin, I can stand up all on my own thank you very much!

Left out mince pie and beer for Father Christmas and carrots for the reindeer. Then went to bed. Later, Mum crept into my room to kiss me goodnight. 'Are you awake, Alistair?' she said. But I was already asleep.

01.15 Slipped out of bed, taking care not to disturb William. Took costume from under bed and the two bulging stockings off the end of his bed and mine. Crept across the landing and found another bulging stocking outside Mel's bedroom door. There was a label tied round the top.

190

Didn't want to wake the baby,
so left it here.
Love,
Father Christmas

I put the three stockings together on the landing for later, went downstairs, got Mr E in from the garden, sat him in the hall and poked some sticks and twigs into his collar until they looked like antlers. Then I fetched the lamp off Mum's desk and positioned it behind Mr E so that when I switched it on it cast a huge shadow on the big wall next to the staircase.

'Now, don't move!' I whispered in his ear. 'You're a reindeer!' Then I went into the sitting room, took a bite out of the mince pie, drank a tiny bit of beer, and nibbled a carrot. I made sure that there were lots of pie crumbs in the fireplace and on the carpet to make it look real. Then I changed into Mr Cloutman's costume and left the room to re-deliver the stockings as Father Christmas.

But as I entered the hall I saw that my reindeer had disappeared. My blood froze, because I knew where he'd be. And sure enough, there he was, with his leg cocked on the unprotected tree, peeing for England! I lunged at him and grabbed him round the throat, which had the effect of turning him off like a tap. What I didn't know, however, was that

192

I couldn't think of a single name. My mind was a blank.

creeping up behind me was Napoleon. While I was busy wrestling Mr E, Napoleon leapt at one of Mum's doughnuts, missed, slipped through the branches and brought the whole tree crashing down on top of me!

The noise brought everyone rushing out of their bedrooms. It was obvious what they were going to think, so they thought it. I tried to pretend I was Santa but it didn't work. 'Yo ho ho,' I said. 'And a happy Christmas Eve to you lot. Have you met my miniature reindeer? He's called . . . erm . . . Mr D.'

No-one believed me. Mum said she was going to put me up for adoption. Mel saw

FOR ADOPTION
(QUICK SALE NEEDED)

Alistair Fury
Likes animals 'cos he is one. Not very housetrained at all.

the Father Christmas costume and screamed, 'Thief! It was you! It was you who got me the sack!'

'Could someone get this tree off me?' I said.

William was still half-asleep and wasn't sure why there was a miniature reindeer in the hall, and Wayne burst into tears when I pulled off my beard. At which point Mary, Andrea and Graham shouted at me for wrecking the magic of Father Christmas for Wayne. They called me a wicked, wicked, wicked, wicked, wicked, wicked wicked boy.

'Could someone get this tree off me?' I said.

'Oh, silent night, holy night
All is calm, all is bright . . .'
Not in Tooting it isn't.

TV MISSED
Oh . . . everything!

DECEMBER 25

YEAH BABY! CHRISTMAS DAAAAAAAAY!

0 days to Christmas

TODAY'S TV
C4, 10.45: Christmas Cop Killers
BBC2, 11.30: Christmas Top of the Pets
ITV, 12.30: Ant & Bee's Christmas Face Pull
BBC1, 15.30: James Bond in Christmas Never Dies
ITV, 18.00: Nicholas Nickleby's Magic Christmas Box
C5, 20.00: Christmas Celebrity Bum Noises
Monster Movie Channel, 22.00: American Peekin' Pie

05.00 Woke early. Fudge to make before everyone else got up. Discovered that William and Mel had been at work while I was sleeping. There was a huge sign at the foot of my bed, which said this:

```
1 •        5 •      9 •
          6 •
2 •       4 •    7 •  8 •
  3 •
```

ALICE, IN YOUR STOCKING
YOU HAVE GOT...

A tangerine
A £2 coin
2 pairs of pants (boxers)
3 pairs of socks
A rude 'Join the Dot' book
2 CDs (Will's already got them and they're rub-
bish)
A fountain pen
A magnet snake
A pencil sharpener
A puzzle
A tube of Smarties (most eaten already)
A fart cushion
Sunglasses
A pair of braces (so nineties)
Handlebar grips for your bike
Coca-Cola flavoured chewing gum
A dead beetle in a presentation case
A book about ghosts
Bubble bath
A wind-up yappy dinosaur

HAPPY CHRISTMAS
Lurve WILLIAM & MEL

* Not slipping it on like a dress, obviously. I mean putting on the turkey in the oven.

It was written so big I couldn't stop myself from reading it. My big brother and sister are fun-knobblers and will pay dearly when I currify them! In the meantime, wrote out list of what was in William's stocking and glued it to the ceiling over his bed so that his awakening would be miserable too, and tied Mel to her bedhead by threading garden wire through her nose-ring and twisting it round a post. Let's hope she doesn't turn over too quickly in her sleep or she'll give herself three nostrils!

While tying Mel to her bed, I heard someone go downstairs. It was Mum putting on the turkey.* When she reached the hall I heard a stifled scream. Crept down to see what was wrong. She was standing in front of the Christmas tree, twisting her dressing-gown cord. The decorations were a bit battered after the fall last night and Action Fairy had broken a leg, but what was upsetting her most was

must... radio... help

the colour. It was Dead Tree Brown. The acid pee had struck again! She rushed past me with a wild look in her eyes, cursing Mr E and Dad, who had it easy lying with his feet up in hospital doing nothing to help *her* cater for *his* family! Then she re-appeared with the hoover and feverishly hoovered up the needles on the hall carpet.

She made such a noise that Andrea woke up and shouted, 'Don't you know what the time is?'

Mum turned the hoover up to full power

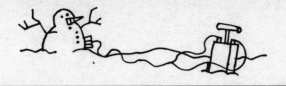

and made even more noise. 'Yes!' she shouted back in a mad, demonic sort of way.

I swear she didn't know I was there. She busied herself around the turkey with butter and bacon and huge sheets of foil and didn't say a word to me. Then she put it in the oven, switched on the heat and went back to bed.

05.55 Locked the kitchen door and got funky with my fiery fudge. I put butter, sugar, evaporated milk and curry powder into a large pan, turned up the heat and

stirred. It wasn't long before I remembered how boring fudge-making was. Twenty minutes later I was still stirring and wasn't allowed to stop till the liquid had started to thicken. Suddenly I heard a crash outside. Objects were falling past the kitchen window. A tube of Smarties smashed into the patio, followed by a bottle of bubble bath and a pencil sharpener ... It was the contents of my stocking!

Raced upstairs to find my big brother and sister dropping my presents out of the window. I tried to jump them and wrestle my presents back, but Mel had longer arms.

'That's for making my nose bleed,' she said.

'And for telling me what was in my stocking,' said William.

'You did it first!' I protested, but this was the wrong thing to say. Whenever William can't win an argument with words he always resorts to fists. On this occasion he held me down and rubbed his verruca over my feet!

BRING ON THE CURRY FUDGE!

Mel smelled the burning first. Then William jumped off me and sniffed it too. 'Maybe it's Dad come back from the hospital,' he said. But I knew exactly what it was.

Mum was downstairs before me. I hadn't been stirring. The fudge pan had caught fire and the flames had spread to the oven. She was spraying the lot with a carpet of foam.

'Wow!' I cried. 'Can I have a go?' It looked really good fun. Except it wasn't. The turkey was ruined and my fudge was as black and hard as coal. As Mum tipped the bird into the dustbin with a slightly hysterical laugh, I chipped a lump of charred fudge out of the pan and, just in case it didn't taste burnt, set it to cool on a plate.

Funnily enough, Mum wasn't as angry as I thought she'd be. She was just glad that nobody was hurt. 'What were you doing?' she asked me.

'Making a secret,' I said. 'It was my Christmas present to everyone.' And now, of course, I had nothing to give. Just as we had nothing to eat for Christmas lunch. I felt bad. Not only had I cooked Mum's goose, but I'd incinerated her turkey as well. And I love turkey!

07.10 Andrea and Graham didn't help matters by announcing how pleased they were that the turkey was burnt, as this would now give them the opportunity to introduce everyone to the joys of vegetarianism.

'You'll love it,' Graham said. 'I used to eat meat, until Andrea explained to me that human beings are actually descended from grass-eaters. Oh yes, cows and sheep. That's why we're partial to nose rings and sheepskin coats, you see. Anyway, it suddenly made sense, didn't it? Why eat meat when grass is so much tastier and free!'

Too much dandelion juice has rotted their brains.

HEAR THIS!

If we get grass for Christmas dinner I don't care what Mum says – I'm down KFC!

08.00 Granny Constance arrived nice and early just in case the photographer from Hello! had stayed the night. 'I have come on the right day, haven't I?' she said, peering around the hall. 'I mean, nothing appears to be ready, Celia. Look at your tree. Has Alistair been climbing it in football boots again? If it was me having my picture taken by the most famous international magazine on the planet, I think I might have made a little more effort.'

'Don't worry, Constance,' said Mum, biting her lip. 'It isn't you having your picture taken. You're not important enough.'

'Oh, I'm sure they'll squeeze me into the back of a few shots,' she said. 'Now, am I too early for a cup of tea? I'll go into the sitting room and wait for you to bring it through, shall I, Celia? With some smoked salmon sandwiches perhaps.'

'No,' said Mum. 'You can lay the table.'

08.25 Under a great deal of sufferance, with much groaning and clutching of her poor back, and comments like, 'In my day it was children who were treated like slaves, not grand-mothers!' Granny laid the table. Meanwhile Andrea grated carrots for lunch and Mum and I sprayed the Christmas tree gold. It was better than brown. Unfortunately the power of the paint spray blew off any remaining needles. In the end, it looked like a large goldfish skele-ton stuck upside down in a bucket.

Eight days ago I'd been looking forward to the best Christmas ever. Since then everything in the world had ganged up against me to make it the worst. I didn't even have presents to give.

08.50 Popped back into kitchen to taste cooling fudge for burntness. It had gone. And standing on top of the plate, looking guilty and licking his greedy little lips, was a small moth-eaten pug dog. The stupid animal had only scoffed the lot, hadn't he? Turbo-bum curry powder and all!

'Good evening, and here is tonight's weather. Strong winds expected in Tooting. Goodnight.'

Suddenly Granny screamed. There was a flapping noise in the sitting room. She said it sounded like a madman shaking out wet sheets. If you ask me, I think there's a madman shaking out wet sheets inside her brain!

As the man of the house and the bravest, William took charge of the emergency and pushed me into the sitting room first in case it was a ghost. There was nothing to see. The noise was coming from the chimney. I was praying for it to be Father Christmas so I could blow a big raspberry at my brother and sister, but it wasn't. It was just a pigeon that had flown

down the chimney to eat the mince-pie crumbs that I'd sprinkled on the floor last night.

'Who left these crumbs?' shouted Mum.

'Probably Father Christmas,' I said. 'His beard gets chock-a-block with crumbs on Christmas Eve and he gives it a good shake every now and then to clear it out. Like an Old English Sheepdog shaking out twigs.' I was told to stop lying. Everyone in the family has always hated me. Now they hate me even more for dropping crumbs.

09.20 The pigeon was nesting in the saggy flaps of loo paper stuck halfway up the hole. We all tried to get it out, but none of us could. Eventually, Mum called a halt when the carpet was ankle-deep in soot. Then Mel refused to hoover it up when Mum asked her, so Mum hooked her little finger through Mel's nose-ring and said in a sweet but deadly voice, 'If you don't hoover, young lady, the nose-ring gets it.'

09.38 Mel hoovered.

She did it in a grumpy, I'm-damned-if-I'm-looking-where-I'm-hoovering sort of a way, which is what led to the accident. First she scared Mr E out from behind the

armchair, then she thrust the hoover in where he'd just been. The squelch sounded like a cake of snot phalumping out of Aaron's nose. The hoover stopped and Mel turned it over to see what had caused the blockage. It was not a pretty sight. It was something Mr E's stomach had manu-factured with the help of the curry fudge. Pug puke! It was beige with coloured high-lights, like a huge wet omelette with bits of vegetable and charcoal in, like minestrone soup with fossils. And it stank like dead flowers. Mel dropped the hoover and ran screaming to the bathroom to take

It was Aunty Andrea having the shave, obviously.

---

a shower, leaving me to clear up with the brass fire-spade and a pair of coal-tongs. It was not easy to pick up and Mr E had done tons of it! As well as Lake Vomit there were lots of little blobs on the carpet, like fairy stepping-stones. They were the size of those gold medallions that American gangsta rappers wear. And it was this thought that gave me the grossest mother of all gross ideas . . .

How was I supposed to know that?! Snigger snigger!

Long dramatic pause.

This will be my finest hour! After today, I will be hailed as the God of Revenge, and big brothers and sisters all over the world will kneel down and worship me with expensive gifts!

09.45 When the doorbell rang I opened it. I was still holding the fire-spade, so the first thing that the *Hello!* photographer saw was medallions of squidgy puke offered up on a brass plate like nibbles at a cocktail party.

'No thanks,' he said, 'I've just eaten. Can I come in?'

'Sure,' I said. 'The dog's just had an accident.' Then I shouted upstairs, 'Mum! The photographer's here!'

After a lot more shouting it was established that no-one was ready and the p h o t o g r a p h e r should wait in the sitting room while everyone had showers and baths and shaves, etc.*

Meanwhile I scraped the puke into plastic bags and put the plastic bags into the freezer.

← Here's the freezer. I'm NOT drawing puke!

Melanie was being a typical girl. Apparently her red tights had been bought specially to go with the red dress that she'd bought specially for the photographs. Now that she couldn't find her tights she couldn't wear the new dress. She was stomping around the house in her bra and pants, kicking furniture and screaming at ME for ruining her life!

How was I supposed to know that?! Snigger snigger snigger!

Andrea was wearing a Red Setter blouse and Graham had on a natty pair of Terrier trousers.

'Not yet!' I shouted back. I asked the photographer if I could look through the viewfinder of his camera.

'So long as you don't take any photographs,' he said.

I promised I wouldn't, then took three of near-naked Melanie with mascara streaked down her face. She looked like the Creature from the Ugly Lagoon! Can't wait to see them in print!

10.15 Everyone came downstairs wearing their best clothes and smiles. The photographer told everyone to act naturally. We should forget he was there, he said, and trust him to record a normal Fury Christmas. When Mum explained about the goose and then the turkey and the tree and Dad being sunburnt and the uninvited guests, and Mel took the opportunity to explain why she was wearing woolly socks under a tatty old dress, the photographer looked a little disappointed, like maybe he should have done Posh and Becks after all, but he promised to do what he could to turn a sow's ear into a silk purse.

Andrea then said that a normal Fury Christmas always involved a little help for the needy. 'Meals on Wheels, Carols for the Bed-bound,' she said, holding Graham's limp hand. 'It's what we always do on Christmas Day.'

'You might,' said Mum. 'But we don't.'

'It would look good in the magazine,' said the photographer.

'Everyone in the car!' said Mum.

But Andrea and Graham don't travel in cars, do they? Unlike normal human beings, they have to walk everywhere or use bicycles or public transport. Have you ever tried to catch a bus on Christmas Day? While we were waiting for one I missed all of *Christmas Cop Killers* AND *Christmas Top of the Pets!*

Sarcasm coming

Still, as long as Andrea and Graham are happy that's all that matters, isn't it? Wait till I give them their present!

12.15 Hadn't crossed my mind that we were going to visit Dad. Hadn't crossed Dad's either. He certainly wasn't expecting us. When we walked in he was tucking into a huge Christmas dinner, swilling the turkey round inside his mouth like it was the most delicious caviare in the whole world. When he saw us, he stopped eating and tried to pretend he was more ill than he looked. He worked his eyebrows up and down to make himself look more pathetic.

Terrible Acting

Then suddenly he froze with fear. He had a Brussels sprout between his lips and gravy dribbling down his chin. 'You haven't got the photographer with you, have you?'

'Oh, I'm sorry,' said Mum with a cruel glint in her eye, 'I should have introduced you.'

The photographer stepped forward and took tons of photographs of Dad trying to hide his face under his sheets and knocking his tray of food onto the floor. Eventually he leapt out of bed, wrapped a sheet around himself to cover his bottom, rushed down the ward and locked himself in the loo. I guess he was camera-shy. Mum seemed to cheer up after that, though.

13.05 Home again. *Hello!* asked for half an hour to set up some lights in front of the Christmas tree.

'Is this the present-giving?' I asked. It was. That gave me thirty minutes to retrieve my ice-pukes from the freezer.

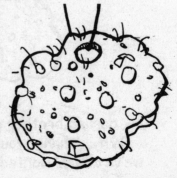

They were as hard as biscuits. I punched a hole in the top of each one, then through each hole I threaded a length of festive ribbon, which I tied in a knot. Then I nicked Mum's paint and sprayed them gold. What a genius I am! Beautiful gold Christmas pendants, courtesy of Mr E's upset stomach! Such a delicate aroma. So perfectly positioned just under the nose . . .

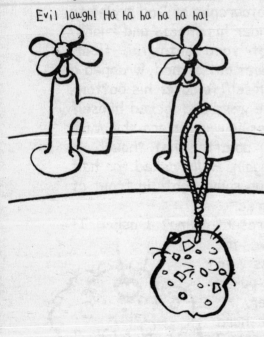

Evil laugh! Ha ha ha ha ha ha!

I was going to make seven p o n g y pendants – one for each of my enemies – but I suddenly had a better idea. The colour of the vomit reminded me of oatmeal soap – the one with bits in. So I made five gold pendants and two soaps on ropes for my darling brother and sister.

'Why, thank you, Alistair. Just what we've always wanted. Pug Puke Soap. It's so soft and creamy!' That's the bile, you idiots! Roll on bath-time!

13.32 Turned freezer up to ARCTIC setting, then popped sick presents back inside for final hardening.

BRRR! ○   ARCTIC ○   ICE STATION ZEBRA ○
COLD ○
BIT CHILLY ○

13.45 Present-giving took place in front of the giant goldfish skeleton with one-legged Action Fairy on top. Because William and Mel thought that they had bought such brilliant presents for everyone they insisted on giving theirs first. Imagine the shock they got when there was nothing inside their boxes! They'd bought nothing for me, nothing for Dad, nothing for Granny, nothing for each other and nothing for Mum. The mood changed. Mum was ashamed of them. Granny Constance moved to a faraway seat on the other side of the hall. Even the photographer said out loud, 'Blimey, that's a bit mean at Christmas.'

that's because she hadn't bought presents either. Her Christmas present to the whole family was her leaving the country for a week!

'It is, isn't it?' I said smugly. 'Not buying people presents at Christmas is like as mean as pushing old ladies in front of steamrollers!'

'I don't mind for me,' said Granny Constance, 'but where are Andrea's, Graham's, Mary's and Wayne's?'

'We didn't know they were all going to be here,' whispered Will and Mel pathetically.

'You are getting close-ups of their shameful faces, aren't you?' I whispered to the photographer. I didn't want my sweet and priceless victory going unrecorded!

'Well,' I announced loudly a few seconds

later, 'even though I did have all my money "stolen" last week, I do have presents for everyone. Not Wayne, I'm afraid, because the presents are small and I know how dangerous small objects can be if a baby accidentally swallows them.'

'Thank you,' said Graham. 'That's very considerate, Alick.'

'So here they are,' I said, producing the gold pendants and handing them round. 'I made them myself.' Got Brownie points from Granny for saying that. 'Do you like them?'

'They're lovely,' everyone said.

'You're meant to wear them day and night,' I said. 'Round your necks, just under your nose!'

'What are they made of?' asked Andrea.

'Stones,' I said. 'Sprayed stones.' How lucky I am that dogs can't speak!

Then I turned to William and Mel. 'Yours are different,' I said, handing them their gifts.

'Why?' asked Mel.

'Because you two are special,' I said. It was time for a little speech. 'I want you both to know that I shan't be bearing a grudge against you for not loving me

219

enough to buy me a present this Christmas – the one time of year that stands for love and peace, when the dove shall lie down with the lamb and the lion with the penguin.'

'Thanks,' said Mel, fingering her dog-made gift. 'So what are they?'

'They're oatmeal soaps,' I said. 'Those bits of grit and vegetables are really excellent for washing your face, and if you drop them in a hot bath, they froth up into the most delicious-smelling bubbles in the world. You can wash your hair with them as well.'

'That's unusual,' said William.

'Yes,' I said, keeping my face as straight

as a poker, 'isn't it? Look, I know it's not much, but it's the thought that counts. And believe me, a lot of thought has gone into your presents. So when you're having a good wash, I want you to think of me slaving away into the early hours of Christmas morning, and think, maybe Alistair's not so bad after all. Because I AM your brother and . . . I DO love you!' I think even the photographer was crying after that. I was brilliant!

Mel and William hung their presents round their necks and said thank you and sorry. Then the rest of the presents were handed out. Will got a Game Boy Deluxe AND a mini-disc player, which was dead cheesy. Mum and Dad had bought me a pool table, which was NOT. I knew it was better than the one I'd bought and William had tricked me out of, because the second

William saw it, he challenged me to a five-frame match – winner takes the new table. I said no.

Like Granny Constance, Andrea and Graham hadn't bought presents for anyone either.

'We don't believe in giving presents,' said Andrea. 'It makes people greedy.'

'Fine,' said Mum. 'Then you won't be wanting our present to you.'

'Oh yes we will!' said Graham. 'We don't mind getting them, do we, Andrea?'

It was round about then that the curry took a further grip on Mr E's gut, only this time it was the back end that exploded into the camera lens. After we'd cleaned up, it was time for a new film and lunch.

THIS PICTURE MADE OUR EDITOR SICK SO WE HAD TO COVER IT UP

Not

14.30 Christmas lunch. What a feast it was.

Andrea had produced grated carrot with a green salad tossed in a light vinegar and embrocation-oil dressing. Nobody had thought to tell her what was in that bottle in the fridge. I had never had embrocation oil on my t o n g u e before. It was like having little boy scouts with blow torches starting fires all over it. There wasn't any wine, because the three special bottles that Dad had bought for Christmas Day had mysteriously disappeared from the cellar.

'What a shame one of us can't change water into wine,' I said as a joke. But nobody laughed. ———————————→ Because they weren't drunk, probably.

And the pudding was a disaster. Mel's tights had run during the steaming, so

_____

apart from having no sixpences inside, the pudding was bright red and sparkly. Mum just burst into tears when she saw it and didn't seem to hear me when I said, 'Oh, Melanie. The sixpences have been stolen and those are your tights inside the pudding. I wonder how that happened.' So nobody got the blame, which was a swizz.

'Never mind,' said the photographer, flashing off another roll of close-ups. 'Give us a smile!'

Wayne gave him more than a smile when Mary changed his nappy on the hostess trolley.

'Did you get that?' Mum asked the photographer.

'What?' he said.

'The dirty nappy,' she said.

'Oh yes,' said the photographer. 'I haven't missed a thing!'

'Oh good!' squeaked Mum. Stress always made her voice squeak. 'I can't wait to see these pictures splashed across the world! Ordinary cookbook-buying people will look at them and think, How normal! Look at those normal Furys enjoying a normal Christmas. I wish I was as normal as them! I know! I'll buy Celia Fury's new Christmas recipe book and look up the recipes for Crispy Green Cack in a Nappy!'

That was the moment I wished Dad had been there. He knows how to deal with Mum when she gets hysterical.

15.15. Wayne pulled cracker in Mr E's ear and ugly pug had second bum-rush on carpet. Mr E was put outside on the pavement. His lead was wrapped around the railings. Mum made up a cardboard sign and hung it round his neck:

He was still there at midnight. I think the haircut we gave him must have put people off. I bet they thought he had mange.

'A DOG IS FOR LIFE, NOT JUST FOR CHRISTMAS.' I AM just for Christmas. Only a few hours to go and I'll be homeless. Take me away with you.

Please!

15.50 The next big excitement brought lunch to a halt. While Mr E was being cast out Wayne disappeared. He'd crawled off somewhere. Andrea, Graham, Mary and Granny ran around the house like the world was coming to an end in one minute. I followed the trail of shredded cracker into the sitting room, where I found the little adventurer sitting on the hearth rug with a mouthful of feathers. Andrea and Graham sobbed hysterically.

'He's only eaten a pigeon,' I told them.

'But he's a vegetarian!' wailed Andrea.

'Not any more,' said William.

16.30 Mary put Wayne to bed, having rinsed out the raw flesh from between his teeth with carrot juice.

16.45 Found Granny Constance on her

knees in the dining room, sniffing the skirting board. 'There's a funny smell in here,' she said, pushing her gold pendant to one side as she leaned forward to smell the hem of the curtains. 'It's sort of sticky.'

17.12 Revengers turned up unannounced to show me their presents. We went upstairs to get some privacy, but William had locked my bedroom door so I couldn't play with my own pool table unless I was playing with him. So we sneaked into Mel's room, where Wayne was asleep, and kept our voices to a whisper. Ralph and Aaron had both got Game Boy Deluxes, which was very lovely for them. When I told them that I'd got another pool table they didn't know how to arrange their faces. Joy or sorrow?

It was Aaron who said, 'I didn't know you were such a pool fan, Alistair. When did it start?'

'When I was too weedy to stand up to Will,' I said. 'I never wanted a table in the first place, but I was scared of saying no.'

'It hasn't been a good Christmas for you, has it?' said Ralph.

I think he was expecting me to agree. In fact I think I was expecting me to agree. But I didn't. Instead I smiled. 'I'll let you into a secret,' I said. 'It wasn't a good Christmas until 09.38 this morning. That was when I found the ingredients to make pendants for the grown-ups, and soap-on-a-rope for Will and Mel.'

'Still don't get it,' said Aaron.

'Well, they weren't pendants,' I said, 'and it wasn't soap!'

'So what was it?' asked Ralph.

'Frozen pug puke!' I laughed. 'It's already starting to stink, and dumbo brother and sister are going to rub it on their faces!'

That was when we heard feet running up the stairs and the three of us dived out of the window to save our lives.

TODAY'S TV
I have no TV.

Have been hiding up the chimney in pigeon's nest for some hours now. Am staying here while manhunt continues. I have something cold and hard sticking into the back of my neck. Don't know what it is. Can't see a thing. It's very dark. Hope this writing is legible.

How was I supposed to know that Wayne's two-way baby alarm was switched on? That everyone in the sitting room could hear me laughing about the ice-pukes! I think I may be up here for some time – like all my life – unless scientists

invent a memory-destroying pill that I could feed to my family. Until then I am not giving myself up. Not even if I discover that I'm mortally ill with a verruca. I have an itch between my toes where William rubbed his disease across my foot. If he has infected me I shall scratch his spots while he's asleep and scab his face all over!

Hang on! Someone's switched on a light. It's getting rather warm up here. Ow! That's hot. Ow! Must move. Agh! Ooh! It's a boot in my neck, with the letters MR C inside. Mr C!? It can't be, can it? Jeepers! That's not a light. It's a fire!

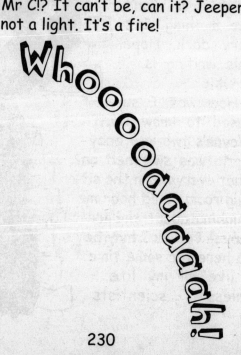

08.30 Ward C, St George's Hospital. In bed next to Dad. Some joker lit the fire last night and yours crispily couldn't stand the heat. William and Mel said they didn't know I was up there, but that is a dispute still to be settled! Luckily I was coughing so much from smoke inhalation when I fell out of the flue that nobody beat me up for the puke pendants. It was as if they hadn't existed. Instead I got taken to hospital, where I am having the best Christmas of my life – no big brother and sister, and the telly's on all day!

Dad says that the boot probably belonged to Mr Chumley, who swept our chimney last March, but I'm not so sure. Why would Mr Chumley have his boots lined with reindeer fur?

16.45 Library lady just came round. Because I'm the youngest on the ward she offered me first choice of magazine. I took today's Hello!, the January issue featuring Celia Fury at home for Christmas. I wonder if Dad is strong enough to read it yet?

WELCOME TO THE HOUSE OF HORRORS!

Have a very Nappy Christmas with Celia Fury!

Oh, fudge! It's a dog's lunch!

Wot? No presents?

Not so 'Ho Ho Ho!' at Celia's ho-home!

Not from his brother and sister...

Who let the dogs out?

Look what Santa brought

Celia Fury's turkey!

Carrot salad – not everyone's choice for Christmas lunch!

Mahatma Gandhi alive and well in Tooting hospital.

Neither is grass!

But Wayne knows what's good for him as he tucks into a delicious Christmas lunch of Chimney-Breast of Pigeon.

Embrocation Oil is Celia Fury's HOT tip of the day!

Followed by Sticky Tight Pudding!

Poor little Alistair tries to win the love and affection of his family. To no avail.

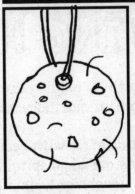

Alistair's beautifully hand-crafted presents, God bless him!

I wonder who'll get the blame for all this? Hmmm . . . can't imagine!

Just in case a Fury torture squad comes for me in the middle of the night, I have made plans for the rest of my life.

MY VERY SECRET PLANS TO ESCAPE FROM MY LIVING HELL

1) Fake death by holding breath.
2) Get taken to mortuary with ticket on toe.
3) Climb into coffin with real dead body.
4) Get taken out of hospital in hearse.
5) Survive overnight in undertaker's fridge/freezer by melting ice with extra-hot sucking mint.

6) Sneak out of fridge/freezer in morning when body-washers arrive.
7) Warm up with nice cup of tea (or hot chocolate).
8) Phone Revengers and get them to pack me some clothes and bring me any homework I might have missed.
9) Have plastic surgery to make me look older (at least thirteen).
10) Forge false papers and passport.
11) Stow away below deck on oil tanker.
12) Jump ship near Jamaica.
13) Swim ashore and make a new life harvesting bananas.
14) Send family a postcard to say that I am safe.
15) Teach myself Big Business stuff by reading in libraries.
16) Buy suit.
17) Make money.
18) Go home for first time in five years.
19) Buy every member of my family a nice car and be forgiven.
20) Sell my story to *Hello!* and only allow family into the photographs if Mum has cooked turkey, Dad is wearing a paper bag over his head, and William and Mel are kissing my feet!

Now that would be a result!

ABOUT THE AUTHOR

Jamie Rix originally started writing and producing comedy for TV and radio, including such programmes as *Alas Smith and Jones*, starring Mel Smith and Griff Rhys Jones, and *Radio Active*. Jamie's first children's book, *Grizzly Tales for Gruesome Kids*, was published in 1990 and won the Smarties Prize Children's Choice Award. Since then he has written children's books for a wide variety of age groups, including *Johnny Casanova – the Unstoppable Sex Machine*, for older readers, and several sequels to the *Grizzly Tales...* This book and its sequels have been adapted into an award-winning television animation series.

Jamie's first book for Young Corgi was the very funny *One Hot Penguin*, which *The Times Educational Supplement* called 'an excellent book with a double-edged resolution'. His latest project is a series of books containing THE WAR DIARIES OF ALISTAIR FURY – the hilarious account of an eleven-year-old boy desperate for revenge on his older brother and sister.

Jamie is married with two grown-up sons and, like Alistair Fury, he lives in Tooting, London.

THE WAR DIARIES OF ALISTAIR FURY

Bugs on the Brain

Jamie Rix

BONSAI! THIS IS WAR

My big brother and sister, William and
Mel, may be older than me and biggerer
than me, but they're not cleverer than me.
Just because the chips of the world are stacked
against me like a potato mountain doesn't mean they can
beat me. Revenge will be mine!

Or rather mine and the Revengers', and a boa
constrictor called Alfred's. Let loose the snakes of
doom and see how they like it then! I shall have my
revenge before you can say 'peanut butter and jam
sandwiches'! Actually I shouldn't have mentioned
peanut butter and jam sandwiches. Forget you ever
read that. If you don't, I may have to kill you.

*The first book in a brilliant and hilarious series by
award-winning comic writer, Jamie Rix.*

CORGI YEARLING BOOKS
ISBN 0440 864763

THE WAR DIARIES OF ALISTAIR FURY

Dead Dad Dog

Jamie Rix

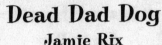

Mum, Dad, William and Mel are ill. It's 'Fetch this, Alistair; bring that, Alistair...' all day long. Huh! Do they think I'm their slave? I'm far too busy sorting out my own problems. First, there's Mrs Muttley and her persistent piano lessons. (I don't know why she won't believe that my fingers have fallen off.) Then there's the bright yellow trousers that my mum bought me – and the photo of me taken without any trousers on at all! To say nothing of Great-Uncle Crawford and the disappearing suit, or Miss Bird and the repulsive recipes...

The only kind ones in this family are the pets – and a vampire dog and an unstable cat aren't much use. Luckily I've still got my real friends – the Revengers – and a ghost of an idea of how to get my own back on the family.

The second book in a brilliant and hilarious series by award-winning comic writer, Jamie Rix.

CORGI YEARLING BOOKS
ISBN 0440 864771

THE WAR DIARIES OF ALISTAIR FURY

Kiss of Death

Jamie Rix

British beef and French mustard
Go together like snails and custard

I know that sounds like one of Mum's gross TV-chef recipes but actually it's a love poem for Giselle, our French exchange girl. *Everyone's* trying to impress her – my brother, William, the Revengers, Colin the builder – they're all after her.

I thought if I said something beautiful to Giselle in French she'd like me best, but I could only think of "Bonjovi, j'apple Alistair". That didn't exactly set her heart on fire... unlike the shed which turned into the barbecue at Mum's boring Bondi Beach party! Me and the Revengers want to throw a proper party with people our own age, kissing and crisps. If Giselle comes to that, she'll be able to see how attractive and mature I am. Ooh la la!

Another hilarious instalment in this brilliant series by award-winning author Jamie Rix.

Corgi Yearling Books
ISBN 0440 86478X